THE GECKO & STICKY
THE POWER POTION

Also by Wendelin Van Draanen

The Gecko & Sticky: Villain's Lair
The Gecko & Sticky: The Greatest Power
The Gecko & Sticky: Sinister Substitute

Shredderman: Secret Identity
Shredderman: Attack of the Tagger
Shredderman: Meet the Gecko
Shredderman: Enemy Spy

Sammy Keyes and the Hotel Thief
Sammy Keyes and the Skeleton Man
Sammy Keyes and the Sisters of Mercy
Sammy Keyes and the Runaway Elf
Sammy Keyes and the Curse of Moustache Mary
Sammy Keyes and the Hollywood Mummy
Sammy Keyes and the Search for Snake Eyes
Sammy Keyes and the Art of Deception
Sammy Keyes and the Psycho Kitty Queen
Sammy Keyes and the Dead Giveaway
Sammy Keyes and the Wild Things
Sammy Keyes and the Cold Hard Cash
Sammy Keyes and the Wedding Crasher
Sammy Keyes and the Night of Skulls

WENDELIN VAN DRAANEN

THE GECKO & STICKY
THE POWER POTION

ILLUSTRATED BY
STEPHEN GILPIN

A Yearling Book

Text copyright © 2010 by Wendelin Van Draanen Parsons
Cover art and interior illustrations copyright © 2010 by Stephen Gilpin

All rights reserved. Published in the United States by Yearling, an imprint of Random House Children's Books, a division of Random House, Inc., New York. Originally published in hardcover in the United States by Alfred A. Knopf, an imprint of Random House Children's Books, New York, in 2010.

Yearling and the jumping horse design are registered trademarks of Random House, Inc.

Visit us on the Web! www.randomhouse.com/kids

Educators and librarians, for a variety of teaching tools, visit us at www.randomhouse.com/teachers

The Library of Congress has cataloged the hardcover edition of this work as follows:
Van Draanen, Wendelin.
The power potion / by Wendelin Van Draanen ; illustrations by Stephen Gilpin. — 1st ed.
p. cm. — (The Gecko and Sticky)
Summary: Thirteen-year-old Dave and Sticky, his kleptomaniac sidekick
gecko, try to keep a special potion from falling into the hands of the diabolical Damien Black.
ISBN 978-0-375-84379-2 (trade) — ISBN 978-0-375-94573-1 (lib. bdg.) —
ISBN 978-0-375-89622-4 (ebook)
[1. Adventure and adventurers—Fiction. 2. Magic—Fiction. 3. Geckos—Fiction. 4. Lizards—Fiction. 5. Hispanic Americans—Fiction. 6. Humorous stories.] I. Gilpin, Stephen, ill. II. Title.
PZ7.V2857Po 2010
[Fic]—dc22
2009028699

ISBN 978-0-440-42245-7 (pbk.)

Printed in the United States of America

10 9 8 7 6 5 4 3 2 1

First Yearling Edition 2011

Random House Children's Books supports the First Amendment and celebrates the right to read.

For the *morrocotudo* Artie Bennett,
who has been one kind and helpful *hombre*.

Special thanks to my editor, Nancy Siscoe,
my partner in fun with whom I share this simple truth:
java junkie monkeys rule!

CONTENTS

Chapter 1
A WARNING

It began as an ordinary after-school afternoon for Dave Sanchez. He pulled on his red Roadrunner Express sweatshirt, clipped on his bike helmet, and pedaled away from Geronimo Middle School to the sneers and jeers of Lily Espinoza and her sassy, saucy girlfriends.

"Hurry, hurry! You don't want to be late, *delivery boy*."

"Have fun *couriering* packages!"

"Don't forget to say please and thank you!"

Dave ignored them and pedaled like mad to put distance between him and his alter-life as a dork. This was not just because it's humiliating and intimidating and incredibly *infuriating* to

1

be sneered at and jeered at by sassy, saucy girls.

Oh no.

It was also because the behavior of Lily and her friends made it terribly tempting for Dave to throw down his bike and say, OH YEAH? and give away a secret so secret that "top-secret" didn't even begin to describe it.

It was more a tippity tip-top secret.

A zippity zip-lip secret.

A spill-the-beans-and-you'll-lose-everything sort of secret.

Fortunately for Dave, he did not spill the beans. Instead, he pushed the pedals. And before long he was downtown, picking up his first delivery envelopes at City Bank.

"Here you are!" Ms. Kulee said, handing him three large envelopes. Ms. Kulee had given Dave his start in the business and took real pride in Roadrunner Express's success. "They're all places you've delivered to before," she said as Dave looked over the addresses.

Dave thanked her and started to move away but stopped and pulled from his pocket a pickup request that had come in from a new customer. "Do you know where Moongaze Court is?"

Ms. Kulee thought a moment, then shook her head. "But I can look it up for you," she said brightly.

"That's all right," Dave said. "I'll just look it up at the gas station."

"Are you sure? It'll only take me a minute to punch it into my computer."

But Dave, being an impatient thirteen-year-old boy, did not have time to waste on what would surely become ten minutes of unexpected interruptions and "quick" phone calls. Instead, he said, "No, that's okay," and hurried out the door and down the steps to his bike.

Dave, you see, often looked up addresses on a map posted in the office window of a gas station that was located in the old industrial part of the city (a route he took to avoid downtown gridlock). It wasn't so much a gas station as it was an old-fashioned service station. One with a tired old dog in the office, a soda machine that held glass bottles, and a side lot full of broken-down cars.

So, after completing his downtown deliveries, Dave rode over to the service station.

Unfortunately, the map posted in the office window was about as old as the axle-greased man who ran the place. "Back again, eh?" the man said as he rubbed his greasy hands on an even greasier red cloth. "Which one's got ya befuddled this time?"

Dave glanced away from the map, taking in the old man's oval name patch. His gray shirts were always the same, but the name patches were *never* the same.

Not yet, anyway.

Today, the old man was Hal.

Last time, he'd been Gary.

The time before that, Fred.

The time before that, Steve.

The time before . . . Well, you get the picture. The point is, there was a body of evidence to support the fact that, despite his consistently axle-greased appearance, the man did, in fact, change his shirt.

No, actually, that isn't the point at all. The *real* point is that the name patch switcheroo was one of the things that drew Dave back to this forlorn service station.

It was a sort of curiosity magnet.

The other thing was the man himself. He was helpful and friendly and seemed to have enough knowledge to span ten lifetimes.

He also wriggled his alarmingly hairy nose when he thought, and seemed to have absolutely no embarrassment about his frequent and flamboyant flatulence (or, if you prefer, firecracker farting).

Perhaps he felt it was part of the full-service gas station experience.

"I'm looking for Moongaze Court," Dave told him, pointing to the outskirts of town on the map. "I found Moongaze Boulevard, Street, Avenue, Road, Way, and Place . . . but there's no Court."

"They do that," the man said. "They keep carvin' up an area and don't have the brains to come up with somethin' creative to name the new streets." He joined Dave's finger on the map's grid with his own, his nose twitching like a rabbit's. "Chances are, it's somewhere thereabouts," he said after a few moments. "That's residential, though. And in Gypsy Town."

Dave looked at him. "Gypsy Town? What do you mean?"

"Ah, well!" the man said, letting out a battery of butt blasts. "Before the city grew and swallowed everything up, gypsies were said to rule that part of town." He gave Dave a sly grin. "If you'd be wantin' your fortune told or your pocket picked, that's where you'd go."

"But . . . I've never even heard of that."

"People are too polite," the man said with a mighty pop out his backside. "Me, I like to tell it like it is."

7

"But . . . *gypsies?* Around here? No way."

"Ah, sonny," the man said with a gentle shake of the head. "Times may have changed, but the ways carry on." He tapped the glass. "If that's where you're goin', be careful."

Still, Dave (being an all-knowing thirteen-year-old) did not believe a word of it. What was a gypsy, anyway? Someone with a lot of scarves and a crystal ball? Someone who could put a curse on you?

Who believed that?

It was like believing in witches or warlocks, and Dave, you see, did not believe in sorcery of any kind.

Which was curious, really, given the nature of his tippity tip-top, zippity zip-lip secret.

But still, he did not.

And so he simply said thanks to the axle-greased man with the changeable name and pedaled away, barreling blithely toward Gypsy Town.

Chapter 2
A POTENTIALLY PERILOUS SITUATION

Gypsies (or, as many prefer to be known, Romanies) are simply a wandering people who (because they were not welcomed into more established societies) learned to survive by telling fortunes, entertaining, and (yes) swindling. A certain romantic air surrounds their reputation, as does an uncertain fear.

This fear is, in large part, a fear of the foreign, a fear of the unknown.

Especially among adults.

Now, as Dave left the main road (named, humorously enough, Jackaroo Avenue) and entered the area the axle-greased man with the changeable name had called Gypsy Town, there *was* a distinct change in scenery.

The roads narrowed.

The sidewalks disappeared.

The houses first shrank, then stacked into multi-storied dwellings with business shingles that dangled from first-floor eaves or awnings and said things such as ALTERATIONS, CLOCK REPAIR, ANTIQUES, and FORTUNES.

The trees grew larger.

Broader.

Shadier.

The ambient temperature dropped.

Slowly.

Steadily.

Dave, however, did not notice these things. His attention was wholly and solely on the street signs. He'd turned left from Jackaroo Avenue onto Moongaze Boulevard, then left again onto Moongaze Street, and left twice more onto Moongaze Avenue and Moongaze Road. And now, spotting Moongaze Way, he turned left *again*.

With each new street, Dave questioned whether he'd made the correct turn. But then he'd come upon the next street, where he would again turn (and again wonder if he'd made the correct choice).

The road at this point was barely wide enough for a car to drive along, and it was here that Dave started noticing goats.

Big, hairy white goats with long, broad horns.

To Dave, they looked like billy goats from a storybook. (They were, in fact, mostly nanny goats, but given their sizeable horns and obvious beards, it was an understandable mistake for Dave to make.) And as he rode deeper and deeper into this Moongaze maze, he noticed them grazing on weeds or nibbling at the leaves of shrubs and trees. One was even *in* a tree. "A goat in a tree?" Dave muttered incredulously (as he did not know that goats are quite good at climbing trees, provided there is at least some slant to the trunk).

When Dave came upon Moongaze Place, he

turned left (again), and after a short ride past more goats (and now chickens, too), he came to a sign announcing Moongaze Court.

Now, this sign wasn't a city-issued green and white metal sign on a tidy metal pole like the rest of the Moongaze signs had been.

Oh no.

It was crudely carved and nailed to a tree, and its arrow shape was pointing to the (you guessed it) left. Moongaze Court, Dave discovered, was not so much a street as it was a narrow dirt path that led to a beautifully painted and ornately carved vardo.

And what, exactly, is a vardo?

It's a horse-drawn home. A nomad's dandy domicile, portable pad, and single most prized possession.

In short, it's a gypsy wagon.

Vardos come in a variety of styles and sizes, and although the one at the end of Moongaze Court was small, it was magnificent. It had a gracefully bowed roof, elaborately scrolled detailing, and quaint, shuttered windows.

Like many vardos, this one was brightly painted (the color scheme here being deep violet, forest green, and gold), and it had four gold wagon wheels—two large ones in back and two medium-sized ones up front.

Handles (similar to those of a wheelbarrow) rested on the ground, and between these handles was a curved ladder that led to a Dutch door.

"Wow," Dave muttered after taking in the scene, "a circus wagon?"

He checked the address against his paperwork, and when he was convinced that this was, indeed, the place he needed to be, he leaned his bike against a tree and approached the door.

Now, Dave had, left by left, wound his way into a potentially perilous situation. There was nobody within earshot. It was as though the surrounding houses had all turned their backs on the vardo, then put up walls, creating a remote area that was isolated from the rest of the neighborhood.

And although there were goats and chickens and large, lovely trees giving the setting an innocent, bucolic feel, Dave was, in fact, in the very heart of what people on the outside called Moongaze Maze.

Now, by "people on the outside," I do not mean people hanging around in their yards, or sitting on their porches, or out for an evening stroll.

By "people on the outside," I mean the people who did not dare (or care) to come inside. People who had heard rumors of gypsy thieves and bad-luck curses.

People like, oh, anyone who lived in a neighborhood north, south, or (especially) east of Moongaze Maze.

People like, say, the mailman, and the UPS driver, and the FedEx guy.

(Even the garbage collectors didn't like going that deeply into the Maze.)

But there Dave was, about to knock on a strange door at the end of a shady dirt path in the heart of a mysteriously mazed neighborhood, completely unfazed by any of it. He was, instead, relieved. Relieved to have found Moongaze Court and relieved to be on his last pickup of the day. (His stomach was protesting the absence of an after-school snack, plus there was the nettling matter of an almost-due social studies project that he had yet to begin.)

And so Dave simply mounted the curved ladder's steps and knocked on the vardo's Dutch door, and a few moments later the top half of the door swung in. A tubby little man with impressively large ears and cloudy, almost white eyes said, "Yes?"

"Yanko Purran?" Dave asked, referring to his printout.

"I am," the man answered.

Dave made his voice as deep and professional-sounding as possible. "Roadrunner Express, here for a pickup, sir."

The man scratched a long fingernail through

the formerly fuzzy blood-red beret that he wore low over his forehead (accentuating his elephant ears). "Very good!" he said pleasantly, and in the brief moments he stepped away, Dave saw the most amazing sight. The vardo was beautiful inside. It had rich wood cabinetry with gilded trim, a bunk to sleep on, and a hand-painted washbasin. But mostly what Dave noticed were flasks bubbling and distilleries dripping and odd-colored liquids in vials.

Yanko Purran returned (blocking Dave's view) and handed over a white mailing tube.

Now, there was nothing alarming or at all ominous about this tube. It was simply a standard cardboard mailing tube with caps on both ends and a label affixed across the middle.

There *was*, however, something both alarming and ominous about the instructions Yanko Purran gave him. "Deliver this to Mr. Black," the man said firmly. "He says that under no circumstances are you to give it over to anyone else at that address. Is that understood? Give it only to Mr. Black."

"Mr. Black?" Dave gasped, and a shiver shinnied up his spine as he saw that the package was addressed to "Monsieur Damien Black, #1 Raven Ridge."

"I said, is that understood?" the man demanded.

"Uh, y-yes," Dave replied, and his voice was neither deep nor professional-sounding. "Give it to Mr. Black, and only to Mr. Black," he repeated.

"Exactly. He wants it by sundown."

Dave nodded, as though in a trance.

"Did you hear me?" the man demanded.

It wasn't until that moment that Dave understood that the man needed to *hear* his responses because he could not see them. "Uh, yes, sir. Of course, sir," he said, this time using his deepest voice. "We'll get it there by sundown."

Well! These were the words that sprang from

Dave's mouth, but these words did not reflect what Dave was actually thinking.

Dave was actually thinking that he'd rather die than go up to Raven Ridge.

Or, more accurately, that he *might* die if he went up to Raven Ridge.

Dave, you see, had been to Number 1 Raven Ridge before.

On several occasions, actually.

He'd had dealings with Damien Black before.

Several times before.

And, to his credit, he'd learned that it was wise to stay far, far away from the diabolical man and his monstrous mansion.

But Dave had never refused a delivery, and before he could grasp the notion that refusal was, indeed, an option, Yanko Purran closed the vardo's door, leaving Dave with the terrifying task of delivering a package to Damien Black.

Chapter 3
GOATS

Dave did not go directly to Raven Ridge.

First (preoccupied with dread over the delivery he had to make), he took a wrong turn as he was leaving Moongaze Maze, and, as I'm sure you know, one wrong turn can easily lead to another. It wasn't long before Dave was completely discombobulated (and hopelessly lost).

Which, of course, caused panic to set in.

And then (as if being discombobulated and hopelessly lost inside Moongaze Maze with a dreaded delivery weren't bad enough) Dave U-turned away from (yet another) dead end and found himself blocked by goats.

A whole herd of them.

Right there.

In the middle of the road.

Plus, he realized with a double take, there was a big goat overhead.

In a tree.

Now, it's a well-known fact that goats eat everything.

That's not to say that this well-known fact is correct, because it's not. Goats are, for example, not carnivores (which eliminates an enormous slice of the pie right there). Nor do they particularly like garbage. Their reputation for indiscriminate ingesting comes more from their curiosity than their culinary preferences.

Goats, you see, are quite intelligent and, consequently, intensely inquisitive. And to satisfy its curiosity, a goat will explore things with its prehensile upper lip and tongue. (These two appendages have, over time, adapted, allowing goats to grasp and hold things.) (And quite firmly,

I might add.) So any consumption of, say, shirts or shoes or delivery-boy bicycle seats is simply the unintended consequence of a goat's need to check things out.

And these goats were clearly intent on checking Dave out.

The circle tightened.

The goats sniffed.

Their top lips pursed and wagged and quivered.

Goat tongues made their way toward Dave.

"Aaaah!" Dave cried (because, really, what else was there to say?).

Now, you may be wondering why Dave didn't just push right through this brash blockade of bearded goats. After all, goats are not predators.

Goats don't circle and attack.

Or stalk and assault.

(They do, it's true, assault stalks, but that's an entirely different matter.)

It was the eyes. The golden eyes with long, slitty, sideways pupils. They reminded Dave of tiger-eyes.

Living, blinking, sideways tiger-eyes.

And tiger-eyes (to make a long story short) reminded Dave of Damien Black, and thinking of Damien Black petrified him.

However, the bleating and groaning and

grunting and baaing that the goats were doing also kept Dave from pushing through them.

Plus, there were horns.

Large, curled horns.

You don't just blithely push through a hard-horned herd of bleating, baaing, grunting, groaning goats.

You just don't.

And *then* Dave noticed that one of the goats had not just two but *six* horns coming out of its head.

Six horns?

Dave was now way beyond discombobulated or panicked.

He was freaking out.

"AAAAH!" Dave cried again, but as he backed away, he rammed right into a second six-horned goat.

"AAAAHHH!" he cried once more, because the goats were now upon him, nibbling at his shoes, his handlebars, his tires, his bike seat, his sweatshirt.

"HELP!" he yelped from inside the herd of side-eyed nibblers. "HELP!"

"Hey!" came a voice from Dave's right. "Hey, leave him alone, you two-toed turkeys!"

It was a girl, no more than eight.

A girl who reminded Dave of his little sister, Evie.

A girl brash and pushy and loud.

One who knew how to get her way.

"Back off!" she said, whacking the goats with a stick. "He's not edible. Go! Go!"

"Thanks," Dave choked out after the goats began retreating, but he felt terribly embarrassed to have been rescued by a little girl. (Especially one so much like Evie.)

"Watch out for Hilda," the girl said, nodding at the tree branch above. "She's a prankster."

As if on cue, the goat in the tree let loose a spray

of pellets, raining little poopy nuggets all over Dave.

"AAAAHH!" Dave cried (yet again) because (yet again) what else was there to say?

He shook out his helmet, then pushed forward, asking the girl, "How do you get back to the main road?"

"Jackaroo?" she asked.

"Yes!" he called over his shoulder (as he was, once again, too impatient to wait for decent directions).

"Second right, right, right!" she called after him.

"*Second* right?"

"Right!" she shouted.

And so off Dave pedaled, escaping Moongaze Maze as fast as he could.

Chapter 4
A THREE-PRONGED FORK IN THE ROAD

After Dave escaped Moongaze Maze, he still did not go directly to Raven Ridge.

Instead, he went directly home.

"Sticky!" he called after he'd made sure his parents and sister were not in the apartment. "Sticky, where are you?"

Well. We've reached the point in the story when I worry about telling you more. Either you already know everything I'm about to tell you or you know none of it. If you know everything, you'll say, Yeah, yeah, I know all that—now get on with the story! And if you know none of it, well, chances are you'll roll your eyes and go, Oh, *right*, and I'll have to jump through a bunch of fast and fiery hoops to convince you that this isn't just some silly make-believe story—that it's true, authenticated, documented, and (in fact) factual.

You see, what I'm about to explain is so unbelievable that not believing it is (I admit) a realistic (and, actually, rational) reaction.

However, I can't go forward without first going back, and so here we are at a little three-pronged fork in our road.

You do, however, have choices, and here they are:

One: If you already know what Dave's tippity tip-top secret is (and what those beans were that he didn't dare spill to Lily Espinoza and her sassy, saucy friends), either read this chapter really fast (so you're sure you're not missing anything you might not know) or just go to the beginning of the next chapter.

Really.

Go ahead.

You have my permission.

Two: Just forget about this story and get on with another one.

(You may find, however, that on the way to doing this, you somehow stub your toe, or run into a doorway and give yourself a bloody nose. Or perhaps you'll have some sort of freak falling incident and scrape up your knee. Then again, maybe none of these things will happen. I'm just saying. For every action there's an equal and opposite reaction. Make decisions in your life wisely.)

Three: Just give me the chance to get this out so we can get on with the story.

So.

You're still with me?

Then here we go with the third prong:

Dave, you see, was much more than a dorky delivery boy.

He was also much more than an all-knowing

thirteen-year-old boy who lived on the seventh floor of a high-rise apartment in a poor neighborhood with one annoying sister and two loving parents.

He was a superhero.

Of sorts.

He didn't wear spandex pants or a fancy cape. What he wore was the ancient wristband of a once fearsome Aztec warrior. (A wristband that, on Dave, fit much better as an armband.)

The wristband itself had no special powers, but when combined with the coin-shaped ingots that clicked into it, it gave the wearer *super*powers. There were ingots for super-strength, invisibility, flying—

But let me stop right there, because the only ingot that matters here is the one Dave had in his possession, and that was Wall-Walker, which gave him the unnatural ability to walk on walls.

Yes, Dave's tippity tip-top secret was that *he*

was the mysterious person known throughout the city as the Gecko.

(As I said, he was a superhero . . . of sorts.)

The other half of the third prong of our fork in the road (and the very tip of his tippity tip-top secret) involves Dave's sidekick.

Of course he has a sidekick. How could he not? It's a well-known fact that *every* superhero has a sidekick. And Dave (or, more accurately, the Gecko) is no exception to this rule.

But being a superhero *of sorts* requires only a sidekick *of sorts*, right?

So perhaps you won't be too surprised to learn that the Gecko's sidekick happens to be . . . *a* gecko.

As in a lizard.

So what good is a lizard for a sidekick?

Well, this isn't just any sidekicking gecko lizard.

This is a kleptomaniacal *talking* (sidekicking)

gecko lizard (who, for the record, cannot explain why he can speak, or why no other animal on earth is able to do the same).

A kleptomaniacal talking gecko lizard named Sticky who stole the ancient Aztec wristband (along with the Wall-Walker ingot) from an evil treasure hunter and gave it to Dave. (So, really, Dave wouldn't be the Gecko were it not for Sticky.)

Now, this treasure hunter did not like to be beaten at his own game, and he certainly didn't like losing his most powerful treasure. This was a man who would never (trust me, ever) rest until he had the wristband back on his deadly, diabolical (and oh-so-dastardly) wrist.

This despicably deceptive man lived high above the city in a monstrous mansion, and his name struck instant terror in the heart of Dave Sanchez.

And his name was (as I'm sure you've already deduced) Damien Black.

So!

Now that we've reached the end of the third prong of the fork in our road, let's get back to Dave and Sticky, shall we?

After all, they have a package to deliver. . . .

Chapter 5
A STICKY SITUATION

Dave did not find Sticky basking in the flower box that hung outside his apartment's kitchen window.

Nor did he find him behind his bedroom bookcase (which was Sticky's other usual spot).

"Sticky!" Dave called again. "Where are you?"

"Over here, *hombre*," came the lizard's sleepy voice.

Dave spun in a circle, looking for his buddy. "Where?"

"Here," Sticky said, emerging from behind the bedroom window's half-drawn shade. "You gotta do something about that crazy *gata*, *señor*. She came at me again with those fishy-hooked feet!

I was taking a nice, sizzly *siesta* in the flower box when—"

"Not now, Sticky. I've got—"

"You don't care that that squooshy-faced monster almost killed me?" Sticky scowled at Dave from the windowsill. "You cut me to the quick, *señor*."

Dave rolled his eyes. "I *care*, but I—"

"She tried to open our window! Ay-ay-ay! You should have seen her!" Sticky clawed his hand through the air. "Rreeeer, rreeeeer, rreeeeer! *Señor,* if she could open our window, I'd be dead right now. You have to do something about her!"

"Right, right, okay, okay," Dave said, producing the cardboard mailing tube. "But first we have to do something about *this*."

Sticky's eyes grew wide as he read the label. (He could, in fact, read, though he had never explained to Dave's satisfaction how he had learned.) "Holy tacarole!" Sticky gasped. He looked at Dave. "You're telling me you have to make this delivery?"

"That's what I'm telling you," Dave said, then quickly told Sticky about the strange elephant-eared man in the strange circus wagon in the strange goat-infested neighborhood.

"Holy guaca-taca-role!" Sticky gasped. And then, after a brief moment of chin tapping, he cocked his head and said, "So . . . what's inside it?"

"How should I know?" Dave snapped. "I don't open the packages I deliver."

Sticky scratched the back of his little gecko neck. "For this one, *señor*, I think you should maybe break that little rule."

"But . . ." Dave shook his head. "Even if I wanted to, I can't. It's got this weird wax seal, see? If I open it, he'll know."

Both caps of the tube did, in fact, have a hardened wax seal dripped over their edges. But the stamp imprinted in the wax was a simple five-pointed star, and as Dave and Sticky studied the seal in silence, they simultaneously reached the same conclusion:

They could open the tube, inspect the contents, and then close it back up and reseal it by reheating the wax and making their own five-pointed star.

Like, with a paper clip.

Or something.

"Do it!" Sticky whispered, as he could see the gears clickety-clacking inside Dave's head.

And so, in a moment of rash impulsiveness (as, no, he hadn't thought through the possible repercussions), Dave pried up one end cap, breaking the wax seal.

Ah, poor Dave.

He had just opened a Pandora's box.

Your classic can of worms.

(Or, perhaps more accurately, a tube of tantalizing trouble.)

"What is it?" Sticky whispered as Dave carefully removed the straw packing material that surrounded a small amber bottle.

The lid of the bottle had a built-in eyedropper, and there was a small note attached to it with a thin piece of twine. The writing on the note was shaky and rough, and Dave struggled to make out the words as he read the note aloud: "One drop. Two at most. Tested. Works."

Dave turned to Sticky. "What do you think it does?"

Sticky shook his little gecko head. "Beats me, *señor*, but if I had to guess? Something evil." He looked up at Dave. "Maybe it's a death potion."

"A *potion?*" Dave frowned. "C'mon, Sticky."

Sticky crossed his arms. "Okay, *amigo*. So what do *you* think it is?"

Dave shrugged. "Maybe some sort of medicine? Maybe that guy was, you know, a medicine man?"

"That black-hearted *ratero* is sick, all right," Sticky muttered, thinking of Damien Black. He considered the situation for a moment, then said, "There's only one thing to do, *señor*—you need to dump it out."

"What?" Dave's face scrunched and twisted. "And then what? I have to deliver *something*."

Sticky shrugged. "Then you refill the bottle with water, put on a disguise, and deliver it to that evil *hombre* like nothing's wrong."

"But . . . when he opens it, he'll know right away that it's water!"

"Look, *señor*," Sticky said with a sharp eye on Dave, "that evil weevil is up to no good. What if he's planning to use that potion on you?"

Dave thought about this short and hard. (He was, after all, under time pressure and didn't have the luxury to think about it long and hard.)

"Okay," he said firmly. "Let's do it."

Instead of dumping the contents down the drain, however, Dave verrrrry carefully un-screwed the eyedropper lid, sucked some of the liquid into the dropper, and then released the liquid drop by careful drop back into the bottle.

The liquid was blue.

A little bit sparkly.

And stinky.

And the drops were very . . . stretchy.

Like they didn't want to let go of each other.

"Soap and Scope," Dave mused.

Sticky had moved up to his usual spot on Dave's shoulder, and held on tight as Dave began zipping around the apartment collecting Dawn dish soap (the original-scent blue) and Scope mouthwash (the blue peppermint variety).

"*Genio* beanio!" Sticky said with a sage nod of his head.

But Dave still did not dump the contents of the amber bottle down the drain. Instead, he rummaged through cupboards until he found a small plastic travel bottle stored in a bathroom drawer. It was empty and had a flip-open squirt top. "This is perfect!" Dave murmured, and transferred the stretchy blue liquid into the travel bottle.

Next, Dave set about trying to match the Moongaze potion. Into a drinking cup he poured (approximately) equal parts Scope and soap, then (after realizing it was too runny) added a generous glob of glue.

When the concoction was mixed up, he pulled out the spoon and watched as it dripped back into the cup.

"*Asombrrrrroso!*" Sticky said. "It looks just like it!"

"It doesn't *smell* like it," Dave said with a laugh, "but who cares?"

Dave filled the amber bottle with his home-made concoction, and when the dropper lid was back on tight, he nestled the amber bottle inside the mailing tube, melted the wax, and resealed the tube's opened end, etching in a star with a paper clip. (He did come dangerously close to starting a fire, but except for the slight charring of one kitchen rug, there was next to no evidence that the seal had ever been broken.)

And then, with an urgent *"Ándale, hombre!"* from Sticky, off they flew to Raven Ridge.

Chapter 6
VINNIE GETS GRILLED

Although one of the power ingots for the ancient Aztec wristband did allow the wearer to fly, Dave (as you know) did not have that ingot. (He would really, really, *really* have liked to have had it, but it was in Damien Black's possession, stashed with other treasures in a cave deep beneath his mansion, guarded day and night by a cantankerous, carnivorous Komodo dragon.)

So! When I say "off they flew to Raven Ridge," I do not mean that they actually flew.

What I mean is, they pedaled really, really fast.

Also, when I say "off they flew to Raven

Ridge," I do not mean that they pedaled really, really fast *directly* to Raven Ridge.

First, they made a little pit stop at the old-timey service station.

The axle-greased man was still going by Hal, and when he saw Dave, he called, "Couldn't find it, sonny?"

"I did," Dave said, swinging off his bike, "but I was hoping you'd do me a favor."

"Sure," the man said with a happy pop out his backside. "Whaddaya need?"

"Can I borrow a station shirt?"

"One of these babies?" the man asked, looking down at his gray and greasy front side.

Dave nodded, then let loose a little lie. "It's for a costume party."

The man's nose wiggled. "So the name don't matter?"

Dave shook his head. "Whatever you've got is fine."

The man led Dave into the office and dug through a heap of shirts mounded on the floor. "No smalls, but here's a medium."

The name patch said VINNIE.

Dave swung off his backpack (and, with it, Sticky, who was watching from the safety of a mesh side pocket). He put the station shirt on over the T-shirt he'd changed into before leaving the apartment and said, "How long can I keep it?"

"Aw," the man said with a scoff, "as long as ya like, *Vinnie.*"

Dave grinned at him as he put his backpack on. "Thanks, *Hal.*"

The old man's backside fizgigged with laughter. "See ya, kid!" he called as Dave pedaled away.

So off Dave zoomed (and sweated and panted and puffed) up, up, up to Damien Black's ominous (and, quite frankly, ugly) mansion atop Raven Ridge.

Now, when Dave operated as the Gecko, he

disguised himself in a very generic way. A ball cap, a bandanna, sunglasses, a plain T-shirt—these were the things he used to conceal his identity. At first, that was because they were all he had or could afford, but the simplicity of the disguise had an unexpected effectiveness:

He looked just like hundreds of other people.

Within the city, debates sprang up as to whether the Gecko was a man or a boy, an executive or a field worker. There were even some who thought the Gecko might be a girl.

Damien Black, however, had seen the Gecko up close and knew:

The Gecko was a boy.

A nasty, nettling nuisance of a boy.

He had also seen *Dave* up close, but (fortunately for Dave) Damien's diabolical mind had derailed before the singularly crucial connection between Dave and the Gecko had been made.

Regardless, Dave knew it would be foolish to

go up to Damien Black's door as himself, or wearing a ball cap or bandanna or even dark shades.

And since Sticky was (as you know) a klepto,
there was often (to Dave's annoyance) a veritable
treasure trove of pilfered items rattling around
inside Dave's backpack.

(Well, some of them, like, say, grapes, didn't
actually rattle. They more squooshed and oozed.)

Dave tried to return things like rings and keys
and watches to their rightful owners (when Sticky
could identify who they were), but his attempted
good deed often led, instead, to a great deal of
trouble.

And so things accumulated.

Rattled 'round.

And sometimes (to Sticky's extreme glee)
came in handy.

"Hey, *hombre!*" Sticky said as Dave scouted out
a safe spot to stash his bike in the forbidding forest
that bordered Damien's property. "You need to

dress gangsta, man. He'll never recognize you. Slick back your hair, wear some bling. . . ."

Dave stopped in his tracks. "Gangsta? *Bling?* When'd you start using words like that?"

Sticky shrugged and went a little shifty-eyed. "You pick things up."

"Stickyyyy," Dave warned, but Sticky was already rummaging through Dave's backpack.

"Here, *hombre*," Sticky said, handing out an earring. Then a chain. Then another earring. And another chain. And dog tags. (Canine, not military.) Next came a pendant with a two-inch rhinestone "M," three rings, and a set of teeth.

Silver teeth.

With sparkly blue stones.

"You stole someone's grill?" Dave gasped, staring at the teeth. "Where did you *get* this?"

Sticky shrugged.

"Sticky!"

"Look, *señor*. If you put on some bling and

I draw some tears by your eye and you wear your pants real low and walk like this"—Sticky strutted along Dave's shoulder with great attitude—"that evil *hombre* will think you're a scary *matón*, not a dorky delivery boy."

"Hey!"

Sticky stopped strutting and shrugged. "I'm just saying. . . ."

"I don't care what you're just saying! I'm not putting someone else's grill in my mouth!"

But even in Dave's state of shock and revulsion, he was aware that he needed a disguise more elaborate than a service station shirt. And then it occurred to Dave that he could rinse the grill with water from the bottle he always carried.

And sterilize it with the hand sanitizer that his mother forced on him.

And then rinse it again. . . .

And so it was that Dave (not having a better

idea) transformed into a gangster named Vinnie, with slicked-back hair, flashes of bling, teardrop "tattoos," and sparkly blue and silver teeth (that didn't fit right and tasted terrible).

"*Morrocotudo!*" Sticky said, greatly pleased with his handiwork. "You look crazy good, *señor!*" Then he added, "I could put some more tattoos on you. Maybe some on the knuckles?"

"Stop it, Sticky!" Dave's eyebrows knit together. "Have you been hanging out with thugs, or what? Is that why you don't want to come to school with me anymore?"

"Ay-ay-ay," Sticky grumbled. "You worry too much, *señor.*" He dropped down on all fours and cocked his head. "So what are we waiting for? *Ándale!* You have a package to deliver!"

So Dave stashed his bike, backpack, and helmet, then took the mailing tube and his delivery folder and strutted out of the forest toward Damien Black's fearsome front door.

Chapter 7
A TERRIFYING TUG-O'-WAR

Imagine tall, heavy oak panels fashioned in the shape of a great, ghastly skull. Imagine hefty brass clackers for eyes and a menacing mail drop for a mouth. Imagine creepy cobwebs and spiders scurrying into darkened corners.

Now you know what I mean by "fearsome front door."

So it's no surprise that Dave's heart was hammering as he clanked an eye-clacker against the whitewashed oak. Especially since he didn't feel at all confident (or, for that matter, thug-like) in his low-slung jeans, teardrop tattoos, and gangster grill.

He felt ridiculous.

"Maybe he's down in the dungeon feeding that killing machine," Sticky whispered from his sneaky-peeky spot inside Dave's service station shirt.

"Shhh!" Dave commanded (partly because Sticky had an uncanny habit of piping up at the wrong time, and partly because he didn't want to think about Damien Black's cantankerous, carnivorous Komodo dragon).

But after another half minute of waiting, Dave grabbed the eye-clacker, and—THUNK . . . THUNK . . . THUNK—he clomped on the door again.

Almost immediately, the mail drop mouth swung back and a furry face peeked through. (Well, the face itself wasn't furry—it was dark with curious brown eyes and a narrow nose bridge—but there was definitely fur surrounding the face.)

"Eeek!" came the animal's voice through the slot.

Dave stooped down to get a closer look, and when the animal shrieked again, Dave caught a distinct whiff of coffee.

"No!" gasped Sticky. "It's that java junkie monkey! He came back?"

Ah, yes.

The monkey.

Dave, you see, had once freed this very same rhesus monkey from a caged existence as Damien Black's personal coffee boy. Damien had (quite cleverly) taught him to brew wickedly good espresso from his rare reserve of outlandishly expensive Himalayan blend, but over time the monkey had developed a taste (or, more accurately, an all-consuming craving) for the coffee himself.

"I guess addiction is a powerful thing," Dave muttered.

"But to come back *here*? That's *loco*-berry burritos, man!"

"Eeeek! Rrrrreeeeeeek!" the monkey shrieked through the mail drop, baring his teeth at Dave.

Dave laughed and flashed his grill right back at him. "Hey, buddy, remember me?" he said (as he had been quite fond of the little imp).

"Are *you* *loco*-berry burritos, man?" Sticky cried, yanking hard on Dave's ear. "Are you *trying* to get us trapped and tortured? He's on that evil *hombre*'s side now!"

Ah, but (despite evidence to the contrary) Sticky could not have been more wrong. The little monkey despised Damien Black and had only returned to kipe the cappuccino.

Make off with the mocha!

Escape with the espresso!

(In other words, he was simply there to jack some joe.)

Unfortunately for the reckless rhesus, he had gotten disoriented inside Damien's maniacal mansion (which is, for the record, an easy thing to do) and had been spotted by Damien Black's resident trio of block-headed bozos, known as the Bandito Brothers. These petty thieves— Angelo, Pablo, and Tito—were not actual brothers but a band of miserable mariachi musicians who went by that name.

Having (in their view) moved up in the world, the Brothers had put music aside and now thought of themselves as Damien's helpful henchmen.

His indispensable assistants!

Or, in moments of deluded sophistication, his protégés.

Damien Black, on the other hand, thought of the Brothers as unrelenting pests. They were like fleas burrowed deeply into the thick, comforting fur of his dark and demented world, and no matter how hard Damien scratched, he couldn't seem to rid himself of them.

And yet the Bandito Brothers were the ones who had spotted the monkey.

They were the ones who had sounded the alarm.

"Boss! Boss, come quick!" Pablo had shouted as they'd tailed the long-tailed intruder.

"Mr. Black!" Angelo had hollered. "Your monkey is back and he's stealing your coffee!"

"Here, monkey-monkey-monkey," Tito had said, holding out a trinket for the rascally rhesus.

But the monkey wasn't interested in sparkly things.

He was interested in coffee.

And so a chase through the mansion had ensued. Out of one room and into another the monkey had raced, with the Brothers in hot pursuit. Up rope ladders and down chutes, along a rail in pulley carts, through a trapdoor, into secret passageways, down one corridor and up another, past rooms with skulls and rooms with maps and rooms with big, dusty books and quill pens, until at last they'd raced round and round and round a combination of confounding corridors where the monkey had finally ditched the Brothers and found his way to the mansion's great room. And this is when he heard something klonking on the ghastly front door.

At this point, the monkey's little heart was pounding in his little monkey chest. He wanted out of that house, and he wanted out *now*. And although he recognized that the enormous skull was, in fact, a door, he was neither large enough nor (despite the double shot of caffeine in his system) strong enough to open it himself.

Then he noticed a smaller door inside the large, ghastly one.

A door he could open.

The mail slot.

"Eeeek!" he'd cried through it, and this "Eeeek!" had, in fact, meant "Help!"

Or, "Open the door!"

Or (more accurately, perhaps), "Get me the heck out of here!"

The hairless primate on the other side had not responded, and so the desperate rhesus had put on his most threatening monkey face and tried again.

It was then (by recognizing Dave's scent) that he realized he knew the person on the other side of the door.

This same boy had rescued him before!

"Eeeek! Rrrrreeeeeeek!" he'd cried, reaching frantically through the mail slot.

So! Now you see that Sticky was, in fact, completely wrong about the monkey. But at that moment it didn't matter, because the eeeking and shrieking had alerted Damien Black (and his trailing trio of cohorts) to the monkey's whereabouts.

"There he is, you fools!" came the evil treasure hunter's voice through the mail slot. "Get him!"

Dave's heart stopped mid-beat, for although he could not actually *see* Damien through the solid oak door, he knew whose villainous voice that was. And in his state of brain-freezing fear, he thought for a moment that the "him" in "Get him!" *was* him.

"Eeeeek! Rrrrreeeeeek!" the monkey implored, reaching out and latching on to Dave's pant leg. "Eeeeek! Rrrrrrreeeeeek!"

This created a through-the-door tug-o'-war, with Dave on one side, a Bandito Brother on the other, and (you guessed it) a monkey in the middle.

"What's he holding on to?" Damien demanded from inside.

"I don't know, boss," Pablo cried, "but he's holding on tight!"

So Dave (wanting to both create a diversion for the monkey and prevent Damien from thinking he had any part in this monkey business) grabbed the eye-knocker and clobbered it against the door. WHACK, SMACK, THWACK! it thundered. "IMPORTANT DELIVERY!" Dave shouted.

There was a split second of hesitation, and then the door whooshed open. (Well, it whooshed as much as four hundred pounds of solid oak can whoosh, anyway.)

Dave (being indirectly attached to the door via a monkey arm) was pulled forward and, in a moment of rash impulsiveness, pretended to fall against the door, shoving it hard. This caused Pablo to lose his balance (and his grip) and allowed the monkey to regain his balance (and release his grip).

Damien had, of course, lost both his balance and his grip ages ago, so he simply screeched, "Catch that monkey!" as the little rhesus escaped the mansion with a small satchel filled with Damien's coveted premium blend slung across his chest. "Get my coffee back!" he commanded the Bandito Brothers. "NOW!"

So while Pablo, Angelo, and Tito charged outside to capture the monkey, Dave stood up and found himself grill to grizzled grimace with Damien Black.

"That's mine," Damien hissed, reaching for the cardboard tube.

"Yo! Not so fast," Dave said, trying to project some thug swagger even though he was feeling quite jelly-kneed. "Wha's yo' name, man?"

"Damien Black," Damien said, taking in Dave's appearance with a disapproving sneer. "Wha's yo's?"

"Vinnie," Dave said with a lip curl, flashing his grill. "Ya need ta sign fo' da delivery." He flipped open the folder and slapped a pen on the delivery order.

Damien hesitated, then grabbed the pen and (with great flourish) signed the paper, then snatched the tube.

Damien took one look at the return address and chortled. Soon little hiccups of laughter were bubbling out of him until, at last, he threw his head back and released a devilishly diabolical laugh. "Bwaa-ha-ha-ha-ha! Bwaa-ha-ha-ha-ha-ha-ha! BWAA-HA-HA-HA—"

"Hey, YO!" Dave said, flipping his hand out. "Delivery charge is ten bucks! And it's a long way up here, so a little extra would be nice, huh?"

Damien's demented laughter came to an abrupt halt as he took in the source of this impudent interruption.

Then, with a sneer and a snort, he simply shut the door in Dave's face.

Chapter 8
STICKY FEELS THE HATE

Dave and Sticky kept their eyes peeled and their lips zipped as they hurried back to the bike, but neither saw any sign of the Bandito Brothers or the monkey.

Once at their hiding spot, Dave quickly removed his bling, grill, and Vinnie shirt, spit-washed off his teardrop tattoos, clipped on his helmet, and skedaddled.

"Yo! I'm Vinnie!" Sticky mimicked as they zoomed down the road. He laughed. "You were *asombroso, señor!*"

Dave laughed, too, and said, "Thanks," but he was still feeling a bit shaky about the whole operation. And after barreling along for a few more minutes, he shouted over the wind, "What if he figures it out? What if he can tell the potion isn't *the* potion?" He glanced at Sticky. "What do you think that stuff does, anyway?"

"I think it does something evil, *señor*. So you did a good thing, okay?" Then he grumbled, "It's that monkey you should be worried about, not the potion."

Now, perhaps you're wondering why the monkey should be of any concern to Dave. After all, the rascally rhesus was surely racing through the forest focused wholly and solely on escaping the Bandito Brothers, right?

The answer is quite simple: The first time Dave freed the monkey from Damien's diabolical clutches, the animal had somehow tracked Dave and scaled seven floors (via drainage pipes and hanging flower boxes) to slip him a strange key (and to brew himself some wickedly strong coffee). What the key unlocked was a mystery to

Dave, and, of course, the monkey couldn't tell him. But it was, without question, a gift of gratitude.

So it wasn't the monkey himself that worried Sticky (although Sticky did not find him to be cute or funny or in any way endearing). What worried Sticky was that the monkey might return and inadvertently lead Damien (or those bumbling, backstabbing Brothers) to Dave's family's apartment.

That evening, as the Sanchez family ate dinner, Sticky worried.

That night, as Dave sweated over his regular homework and his social studies project, Sticky worried.

All night, as Dave snoozed and snored and drooled, Sticky worried.

By morning, however, there'd been no eeeking or shrieking (or mysteriously brewed coffee). And so, as the Sanchez family went through their

usual get-to-school-on-time routine (involving gobbled food, spilled milk, hastily packed
lunches, and a lot of hurry-it-upping), Sticky fell
fast asleep.

"Psst!" Dave whispered behind his bookshelf
when he was ready to go. But try as he might, he
could not convince Sticky to get up, so, at last,
he gave up. "Just stay out of trouble, then, okay?"
he whispered, and raced off to school.

Now, had Sticky slept through the day, this
would not have been such a tall order. Unfortunately, at around noon, Sticky woke up hungry.

Very hungry.

And so he went outside through the kitchen
window (which was, for ventilation purposes,
always left open an inch or two) and spent an
hour or more hunting down such delicacies as
meaty-legged grasshoppers and mealworms.

Then, feeling fat and quite happy, he scaled
back up the wall to the Sanchezes' flower box and

settled in for a nice, bone-warming bask in the afternoon sun.

Next door, Topaz the cat sat inside on the windowsill and watched.

"Hey, uuuuugly," Sticky called with a stretch and a yawn, for he was safe from the squooshy-faced terror, as today the Espinozas' window was also only open about an inch.

Topaz's long white tail twitched, and her tiger-like eyes zeroed in on Sticky.

She began pacing along the windowsill.

Back and forth, back and forth.

She added mewing.

Pitiful, plaintive mewing.

Topaz was, by nature, an ill-tempered cat. And being on house arrest day and night did nothing to improve her disposition. She had little to do but sulk on the windowsill *wishing* for something to do. (Or, more precisely, something to stalk and kill.)

Mice in the building would have been nice.

Instead, there was a lizard.

A teasing, taunting, exasperating lizard.

One with a big, fat (and decidedly delicious-looking) tail.

Ah, poor Topaz.

She hated her plight.

Hated the monotonous (and often stale) kibble Lily left out for her.

Hated being alone all day.

Most of all, though, she hated the lizard.

Now, this was not because she understood "uuuuugly" when Sticky called her that. She was, after all, a cat, and cats don't actually understand words.

Tone and sound, yes.

Words, no.

Her fenced-in feeling was what started the cat's obsession with Sticky, and his taunting just added fuel to the feline's fire. She watched for him day in and day out, biding her ill-tempered time, pacing away the hours, hoping that someday, someway, she could escape her glass prison and catch him.

Now, had Topaz simply sat in the window, none of what I'm about to tell you might have happened. But Topaz didn't just sit. Topaz hissed and paced and pawed and clawed, futilely reaching her long hooked nails through the opening in the window.

Sticky, as you might imagine, could feel the hate.

And feeling all that hate gave him a very naughty idea.

One he mistook for an *asombroso* idea.

One that got him up and running lickety-split into the Sanchezes' kitchen, where he scraped together a nice little ball of leftovers from the bowl Mrs. Sanchez had used to mix up tuna for Evie's and Dave's lunchtime sandwiches.

One that involved fetching the hidden bottle of Moongaze potion and dripping two careful drops of it onto the tuna ball.

One that had Sticky scurrying over to the Espinozas' flower box with the tuna on a white plastic spoon.

An idea that would, I'm afraid, show him just how potent and dangerous the pilfered potion could be.

Chapter 9
OPENING THE POWER GATES

Topaz went into a rage when she saw Sticky on her flower box. Her long white fur shot straight up, then she swiped and hissed and scratched and (in short) went ballistic.

Until, that is, she caught a whiff of the tuna.

"Atta crazy *gata*," Sticky said, coaxing Topaz along. He had the plastic spoon under the window and was jiggling it to get the ferocious feline's attention. "It's yummy to the tummy—come on. . . ."

Topaz's fur slowly descended.

Her nose twitched over the fish.

Her whiskers quivered.

And then, forgetting all about the maddening

fat-tailed lizard outside, she quickly devoured the potion-laced fish that was inside.

Sticky watched.

And waited.

But the potion seemed to have absolutely no effect.

"Ay-ay-ay," Sticky grumbled. "It's a dud." He frowned. "Or maybe it just doesn't work on ugly cats."

Topaz, too, seemed disappointed. After all, the tuna was gone.

Now, a stable cat might have mewed for more.

A stable cat might have remembered who'd brought the tasty treat.

A stable cat might have repaid the gift giver by showing him a little kindness. (Or, at least, aloof indifference.)

But Topaz was not a stable cat.

She was an angry cat.

One whose appetite for meaty morsels had just

been whetted and was now focused on the mouth-watering morsel taunting her from just outside her glass prison.

One who, at that moment, clawed through the opening with an angry hiss and, to her surprise, felt the window edge upward.

Now, for all the times Topaz had reached for Sticky, the window had never (believe me, ever) budged. Feeling it move now gave the frustrated feline hope, and after a short disbelieving moment she pushed farther.

To her delight, the window, once again, edged upward.

She really put her shoulder into it now, and the window edged upward some more!

Flashing through Sticky's mind was one simple thought:

"Uh-oh!"

And before he had even zippy-toed over to the Sanchezes' flower box, Topaz had strong-armed the window up and was charging after him.

"*Ay caramba!*" Sticky cried as he scurried under the Sanchezes' window.

Ay caramba, indeed!

The potion, you see, had not changed Topaz's appearance (or disposition) in any way, but it had, in fact, given the cat an unfamiliar strength.

Now, I'm sure you've heard of incidents in which a mother somehow lifts a car to save the life of her child. Well, let me assure you that these stories are not tall tales or urban legends or (to put it less delicately) lies.

They are actual, factual (and impartially documented) events.

(Incredible, perhaps, but still, actual and factual.)

You see, scientists speculate that within the body (be it human, cat, or lizard), there are inhibitors that prevent you from exerting yourself to your full physiological potential. (In other words, there's always "superhuman" strength inside your body, but gates at the power source block it.) A crisis (such as a child pinned by a boulder or a car or a runaway Ferris wheel) triggers the gates to open, providing the body with an unfamiliar (and seemingly superhuman) strength.

So! Although the Moongaze potion was slightly sparkly and surprisingly stretchy, it was not some magic concoction or hocus-pocus potion.

Please.

It was a complex cocktail of rare and exotic ingredients (collected by gypsies in a remote region of eastern Romania), and it simply opened the body's natural power gates, supplying a seemingly superhuman strength.

Unfortunately for Sticky, Topaz immediately realized that she was now more tiger than cat.

More fierceness than fur.

More power than purr.

And she was, as they say, lovin' it.

"Reeeeeerrrrrr!" she roared as she ripped open the Sanchezes' window and pounced inside the apartment. "REEEEEERRRRRR!"

"Holy guaca-tacarole!" Sticky cried, turbo-toeing out of the kitchen.

And so the chase began.

Topaz tore through the apartment like a wild-whiskered twister. Out of one room, into another, under furniture, over furniture, through plants, and across the TV she flew, knocking things over left and right. And

even when she realized she had lost track of the lizard, Topaz continued tearing the place apart, upturning chairs, ripping through cupboards, tossing aside cushions like a fur-faced tornado.

It was, I assure you, a frightening sight. And although Sticky had escaped the hissing hurricane for a moment, Topaz now spotted him on the family room ceiling.

"RRRRREEEEEERRRR!" she cried, charging up the wall, leaving scratch marks in her wake. And when she couldn't reach Sticky that way, she launched herself skyward from furniture backs, clawing and hissing at her target as she sailed through the air.

Try as she might (and she did, in fact, try mightily), she could not reach Sticky. (Although she did, at one point, manage to sink her claws into the ceiling a mere two feet from him and hang there for a solid minute before dropping to the floor.)

And then, all at once, the power gates slammed shut.

Topaz was back to being Topaz—an average, ill-tempered, squooshy-faced cat.

Poor kitty-kitty.

She was, of course, confused.

After mewing pitifully from the floor beneath Sticky for almost an hour, she at last grew weary (and, undoubtedly, thirsty and hungry) and skulked out of the ravaged apartment, hopping flower boxes to return home.

This was a great relief for Sticky. However, before he could scurry back to the kitchen to collect the Moongaze potion, a sound from outside stopped him in his tracks.

"Ay *caramba*, no!" Sticky gasped. "Not him!"

But it was, in fact, just who Sticky feared.

Chapter 10
A QUICK BACKTRACK

Since Sticky has stopped in his tracks, perhaps this would be a good time for us to do the same. After all, I'm sure you're wondering what happened to the monkey.

And the Bandito Brothers.

And, for that matter, Damien Black.

Yes, of course you are.

You're probably also wondering if Damien Black was already trying to launch some deadly, diabolical plan with Dave's substitute potion.

These are, after all, perfectly legitimate things to be wondering.

So let's start with the monkey, shall we?

Getting away from the bumbling Bandito

Brothers was really quite easy for the rascally rhe-sus. The forest surrounding Damien's mansion was dark, and dense, and (without question) danger-ous. (Also, once inside, it was difficult to navigate, especially for the directionally impaired.)

Monkeys, however, are right at home in forests, and (despite years in Damien's captivity) this little monkey was very comfortable scamper-ing and swinging from tree to tree with his satchel of stolen coffee. He simply led the Brothers deeper and deeper into the dark and dangerous forest, screeching, "Eeeeek! Reeeeeeek!" as he scurried from branch to branch above them.

"There he goes!" Pablo cried (over and over again) as they tracked the monkey. "Get him!"

"How am I supposed to get him?" Angelo snapped (over and over again) as he struggled to keep up. "He's in a tree!"

"Here, monkey-monkey-monkey!" Tito called, holding out an apple he'd had in his pocket.

Now, while Tito (simpleminded as he was) was happy to be tracking a fuzzy-wuzzy monkey through the forest, Angelo and Pablo knew that returning to the mansion without the rhesus (or, at least, the coffee) would be a bad move.

A *very* bad move.

Damien, you see, was prone to bad moods, and bad *moves* (such as failing to catch a runaway rhesus) usually resulted in a lot of shouting and routing and accusations of flouting, and (after Damien had worked himself into a spitting, sputtering rage) threats of horrifying torture and death.

And so the Brothers chased the monkey deeper and deeper into the dark and dangerous forest, until at last the monkey grew weary of the little game.

"Eeeeeek! Rrrrreeeek!" he screeched from the branches of a gnarly pine tree. "Eeeeeeeek! Rrrrrreeeeek!" Then he began pelting the

Brothers with sharp, sticky (and extremely sappy) pinecones.

"Ow!" Pablo cried, trying to duck away from the monkey's deadly aim.

"Yow!" Angelo yelped as he got pummeled.

"Play with *me*," Tito laughed, throwing his apple at the rhesus.

"Eeeek?" the monkey said, catching the apple and rifling it back, landing a painful bonk on Tito's head.

The monkey then scurried off, and after a few minutes of Brotherly fighting (which sounds very much like the fighting of real brothers), Angelo, Pablo, and (even) Tito came to the frightening revelation that they were lost without water or food or (even more urgent) toilet paper in a dark and dense (and obviously *dangerous*) forest.

The solution to this was, of course, to resume fighting.

Meanwhile, back at the mansion, Damien

Black was wasting no time in trying out the potion. "Bwaa-ha-ha!" he laughed (for he knew full well what the potion would do). "Bwaa-ha-ha-ha-ha!"

He entered his great room with a *whoosh-swoosh* of his long black coat and settled into a large throne of a chair that had deep, dusty cushions and great carved gargoyles perched on the backrest. "Ah!" he said with a contented shudder. "Bwaa-ha-ha-haaaaah."

Damien then spritzed open a bottle of chilled Armenian pomegranate juice (his favorite thirst-quenching beverage) and placed it at the ready on an ornately carved end table.

Then, with great flourish, he stuck out his long (and, for the record, unusually pointy) tongue and dripped onto it one . . . two . . . (what the heck) *three* drops of the potion.

Saliva swirled with the potion in his mouth as Damien tried to analyze it with his taste buds.

It was rather pungent (but with a hint of mint).

Oddly bubbly.

Strangely . . . sticky.

Yes, he decided with a shiver, it was a bit icky-sticky, but that was to be expected, right?

This was, after all, a powerful potion, not some swishy champagne!

And so he swallowed it and chased the now foamy potion down with a satisfying swig of pomegranate juice.

Then he waited.

And waited.

And waited some more.

Now, although Dave had poured the Moongaze potion out of the amber bottle, he had not rinsed the bottle. And since the real Moongaze potion was quite viscous (or, if you prefer, ooey-gooey), an ample sample had, in fact, clung to the walls of the amber bottle and, over the course of the thumpity-bumpity bike ride up to Raven Ridge, had mixed in with the soap and the Scope (and the generous glub of glue).

And so, as Damien waited, the watered-down (or, really, soaped-up) potion did work.

A little.

Damien lifted the side table, and although it was considerably easier than it would otherwise have been, it was nothing to bwaa-ha-ha about.

After a few more impatient minutes of waiting for something big to happen, Damien once again stuck out his pointy tongue and dripped onto it one . . . two . . . three . . . *four* more drops.

Again, he waited.

And waited.

And waited.

And again, the change in him was disappointing.

His glinting black eyes grew angry, and this time he *doused* his tongue with the potion.

He waited again, then did it again.

And again!

"That miserable charlatan!" he hissed after the potion still failed to give him superhuman strength. "He gypped me!!"

Unfortunately for Damien, the substitute potion *was* having an effect on his system. Soap, you see, is a surfactant. It works by lowering the interfacial tension between liquids. (In other words, it breaks down the forces that attract molecules to each other. Like, say, someone with awful onion breath joining a conversation. Only at the molecular level. And with liquids.)

Now, the effect of soap on the human intestinal system varies in degree from person to person, but it acts, by and large, as a laxative.

It loosens your stools.

Gurgles your guts.

And (let's just be frank, shall we?) makes you go poo-*poos*.

And so it was that Damien Black wound up trading his gargoyled throne in the great room for a porcelain one in the bathroom.

And while his guts gurgled and sputtered and rattled inside him, he began plotting ways to pay back that swindling gypsy.

He wouldn't take this sitting down! (Although

he was, at the moment, doing just that.)

He would get his revenge!

Somehow, he would!

Bwaa-ha-(gurgle-gurgle)-ha!

Chapter 11
SUCKEROOED

There was nothing swift or sharp about Damien's revenge.

He was, after all, hampered by sudden bouts with his bowels that demanded frequent (and frantic) trips to the loo.

Ah, but skip-to-my-loo'ing aside, Damien was even more hampered by superstition.

You see, Damien Black was afraid of gypsies.

(He wasn't afraid of much, but gypsies? Oh my.)

They gave him the heebie-jeebies.

The snaky-spined creepies.

The not-so-nilly willies.

(This, for the record, was a direct result of having once been on gem safari in Bulgaria, where he'd planned to do a diabolical double cross and steal the legendary Romany ruby but had, instead, been cursed and conned and run out of town by gypsies.)

Yes, the simple truth is, a fear of gypsies was what had prevented him from going down to Moongaze Court to pick up the potion himself. A fear of gypsies was what had caused him to spend so much time on his custom-built funky-doodle phone, pinching an inordinate amount of broadband as he tracked down a courier service to pick up the package for him.

Now, by "pinching," I do not mean that he squeezed it between his long, pointy fingers.

Oh no.

By "pinching," I mean that Damien did not pay for his phone service.

He had simply run lines from his house to the nearest phone-company box and cleverly (and quite surreptitiously) wired his way into the system.

He did not piggyback onto someone else's service either. Instead, he wired directly into the phone cable trunk, creating a line on which he could call out but (as there was no actual number) no one could call in—something that suited Damien just fine.

(A word of caution: Should you ever check the caller ID on your ringing phone and discover that the display shows nothing at all, beware. It could well be Damien Black on his funkydoodle phone, calling with a list of diabolical demands.)

And what, exactly, is a funkydoodle phone?

It is, in short, a typical Damien Black contraption. Rather than spend twenty bucks on a perfectly functional drugstore model (because it would clash with the mansion's dark and foreboding décor), Damien had constructed his own. The handset was an interlocking ancient ivory ear horn and taxidermied eagle's claw (which held a cheesy speaker in place). The base had a rotary dial that was made out of ten fossilized shark vertebrae. (The phone also had a duplex coil and a frequency generator for functionality, but no matter—it was, without doubt, one funkydoodle phone.)

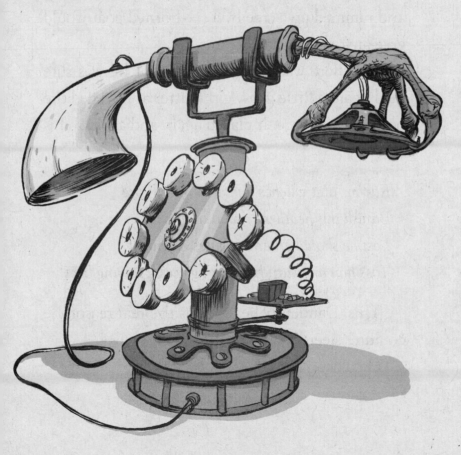

So you see, Damien Black had gone to great lengths to avoid Moongaze Court. His one trip there to arrange for the potion had left him battered and weak, and had given him nightmares for weeks. (I'm sure you'll agree that being cornered and rammed up a tree by a six-horned goat would give anyone baaaaad dreams.)

But there was also the curse that he was sure he'd heard a little gypsy girl mutter as he'd fled the nightmarish maze. It played again and again in his head:

Ravens and witches and demons of yore,
Banish this heathen from our door!
Lest he should enter our gates o'ernight,
Toss him and turn him through wick's dying light!

This, Damien believed, was the real reason he couldn't sleep.

He'd been cursed.

Again.

The Bulgarian curse still haunted him, and now this?

He would not, could not, return to Moongaze Maze.

And yet . . . what about his revenge?

He had a score to settle!

A wrong to right!

He'd been duped!

Swindled!

Suckerooed!

(And of all the deceitful, duplicitous, double-dealing things someone could do to him, suckerooing was by far the worst.)

And so (between great gurgling bouts in the bathroom) he consulted large, scrolled maps of the city, more large, scrolled maps of the underlying sewer system, and dusty, crumbling texts from the massive oak bookcases in his great room.

His dark, diabolical mind stewed and brewed

and chewed until at last it produced a wickedly delicious plan.

"Bwaa-ha!" he chortled. And as he paced the floorboards, he began seasoning his plan with a dash of evil here and a shake of vengeance there, until at last he began muttering, "Where *are* those buffoons? What is taking them so long?"

Yes, for the first time since they'd blundered into his life, Damien Black wanted the Bandito Brothers to be there.

His devilish plan required the Brothers.

They were, after all, delectably disposable.

And if all went well, *they'd* be the ones cursed, and that deceitful, duplicitous, double-dealing gypsy would be the one suckerooed!

Chapter 12
THE WINK OF A WICKED EYE

So! Now that you know what happened up on Raven Ridge, let's quit stopping in our tracks and get back to Sticky and the sound he heard, shall we?

It was, as you may recall, a sound Sticky recognized.

One that was worse (much worse) than the hissing and spitting of a turbocharged cat.

"Reeeek?"

Sure enough, a satchel-toting monkey swung in through the Sanchezes' kitchen window.

"*Ay caramba*, no!" Sticky cried, moving lickety-split across the kitchen ceiling. "Out! Leave! *Vámonos!*"

The rhesus simply bared his teeth at Sticky and ambled across the counter toward the coffeemaker.

Now, I'm sure you're wondering why (given all the coffeemakers in all the kitchens in the city) the rhesus came to Dave's apartment to brew his coffee.

It is, after all, a perfectly reasonable thing to be wondering.

The answer is (again) quite simple: Monkeys are creatures of habit. (Although, in this case, things were slightly more complex, as this monkey was a creature of habit *with* a habit.)

You see, aside from Damien Black's house, the only place the little rhesus had actually brewed coffee was the Sanchezes' apartment. And in the days since his last swing through the Sanchezes' kitchen window, the little monkey had survived by snatching to-go cups from coffeehouses, haphazardly lifting straight brews, lattes, mochas, and double shots (with the occasional *pttttth*-inducing chai).

And despite cries of "Hey, that's my coffee!" and "Excuse me. . . . Ex*cuse* me . . . !" and (simply) "Stop that monkey!" he'd managed (for the most part) to avoid the debilitating headaches that are characteristic of caffeine withdrawal.

Still. Jacking to-go joe was a lot of work. And dangerous. Plus, nothing he'd snatched compared to Damien's Himalayan blend.

So now that he had a supply of the good stuff and a coffeemaker within reach, the rhesus wasn't going to let a little thing like an angry lizard stop him from brewing a wicked good cup of coffee.

"Reeeeeeek!" he warned Sticky, baring his teeth again.

It was clear to Sticky that there was no reasoning with this rhesus.

It was also clear that there was no fighting

him. With opposable thumbs, a long, agile tail, and a killer craving for coffee, the furry beast was just too fearsome a foe.

But as he watched the rhesus slam through drawers and cupboards for a filter, a mug, and a spoon . . . as he watched the coffee sputter and steam and then stream into a waiting mug, an idea formed in Sticky's little (but very powerful) gecko brain.

It was, as you might already be guessing, yet another very bad idea.

One that involved a certain potion that was still sitting on the counter near the coffeemaker.

"Ay-ay-ay," Sticky muttered, and although "ay-ay-ay" can mean many things (or, on occasion, nothing at all), this "ay-ay-ay" meant one clear, specific thing:

"Do I dare?"

Ah, poor Sticky.

He was flirting with temptation.

In his head, a little voice was telling him that if he had a minute of super-strength—just one little minute—he could fling that monkey right out the window.

Adiós, monkey nose!

And . . . if he had *another* few minutes, he could lickety-split straighten things up quick before anyone came home.

And . . . if he had just a few *more* minutes . . .

Yes, this is what happens when you flirt with temptation—temptation is happy to flirt right back. In the wink of its wicked eye, you find yourself reaching for the potion, telling yourself you'll only use it to help you through this bad situation, swearing you'll only take one drop (or maybe, at the very most, two).

Unfortunately (or fortunately, depending on how you look at it), the monkey had been keeping a wary (and now re-caffeinated) eye on the lizard. So perhaps it was the way Sticky was approaching the bottle.

Or the obvious intensity of Sticky's mission.

Or perhaps the monkey was just in a playful mood.

Regardless, the little rhesus seemed to sense what Sticky was after, and with a playful *swoosh-*

snatch he scooped up the little bottle of potion and smiled. "Reeeek?"

"No!" Sticky cried as he scampered up the monkey. "Give it back, you *bobo* baboon!"

The monkey gave him an insulted look, then simply shook Sticky off as he leapt onto the kitchen floor. "Reeeeek?" he said, wagging the bottle at Sticky.

Sticky knew that chasing the monkey would be, as he would say, *estúpido*.

So instead, he tried to outsmart the rhesus.

He zippy-toed across the counter and dragged a banana from the fruit bowl. "Here, monkey-monkey-monkey," he said, hoping the monkey would just drop the bottle and take the bait.

Instead, the monkey tucked the bottle inside his satchel (which was still slung across his chest) and *then* snagged the banana.

"You *zonzo* Bonzo," Sticky muttered, but

when he tried to retrieve the bottle from the satchel, the monkey simply leapt to the floor again.

"Reeeek?" the monkey said. He bared his squishy-banana teeth and made a laughing noise, then scampered around the corner toward the bedrooms.

"What the jalapeño am I going to do?" Sticky cried as he zippy-toed after the rhesus. When he caught up to him, he found the monkey leaping around Dave's room, tearing things up, tossing things around, making an eeky-shrieky mess of the place (as naughty, hopped-up monkeys are prone to do).

"Freaky *frijoles!*" Sticky cried. "Get out! Go! *Ándale!*"

But the monkey had discovered a stash of shiny objects, including the grill Dave had worn to make the Raven Ridge delivery. He cocked his head and inspected the silver and blue teeth. "Eeeek?" he asked softly.

Suddenly there was a noise at the front door.

The monkey froze.

His eyes went wide.

His mouth pushed out into a little "oo." (Or, perhaps more accurately, a little "uh-oo.")

And in a furry flash, he scampered into the kitchen, leapt onto the counter, took one last (extremely satisfying) gulp of coffee, then swung outside onto the flower box and escaped.

Chapter 13
WELCOME HOME

It was Dave who fumbled through the front door, famished and exhausted and just glad to be home. He'd been up half the night working on his social studies project, he'd had to run the mile twice in P.E. (once for health and once because Eli Unger had stolen Mr. Wilson's whistle and nobody dared fink), and his after-school deliveries had taken him to far ends of the city (although, thankfully, to neither Moongaze Court nor Raven Ridge).

Dave needed food!

Rest!

(And, of course, to get going on his homework.)

Instead, he got a topsy-turvy house that smelled suspiciously of Himalayan coffee.

He pushed his bike farther inside, calling, "Mom? Dad? . . . *Evie?*"

There was, of course, no response from any of them, as Evie spent her after-school hours with her mother at the Laundromat where Mrs. Sanchez worked until five, and Mr. Sanchez rarely arrived home before six.

The response came, instead, from Sticky. "It was that crazy *gata!*" he cried, racing toward Dave. "And the monkey! It's a miracle I'm alive! I *told* you that fuzzy-faced monster was trying to kill me!"

"But . . . ," Dave gasped, looking around at the damage. "Topaz *and* the monkey? How did they get in?"

Sticky shot up to his familiar place on Dave's shoulder. "The window!" he said, pointing.

Dave (certain that his parents would blame *him* for the chaos) began cleaning the kitchen.

"So the monkey opened the window and then Topaz came in?" Dave asked, trying to come to grips with what had happened as he picked up the half-eaten banana.

"I tried to stop them, but what can one lizard do?" Sticky asked (neatly avoiding the question).

Dave was still stunned. "They were here at the same time?"

"*Horroroso* exploso!" Sticky moaned. "Monsters everywhere!"

"This place is a disaster!" Dave groaned, moving into the family room. "How long were they here?"

"A lifetime!" Sticky cried. Then (very slyly) he added, "The minute they heard you at the door? Zippity-doo-dah, they were gone!"

"So they *just* left?"

"*Sí, señor.*"

Dave was righting the furniture in the family room when he noticed the scratch marks on the wall and the claw marks in the ceiling. "How in the world . . . ?"

"That cat went *loco*-berry burritos trying to get me! *Now* do you believe me?"

Suddenly Dave was mad. Lily's cat *was* a beast! She really could have caught and killed Sticky!

He also suddenly felt guilty. Why hadn't he paid attention to what Sticky had been saying about the cat? He'd been complaining about Topaz for weeks.

Now, a calm, collected person would have realized that a normal cat (ill-tempered or otherwise) could not possibly have created such chaos. But Dave was neither calm nor collected. He was shocked, stunned, and now angry.

And so it was that Dave took Sticky at his word and marched out of his apartment and pounded on the Espinozas' door.

A short minute later, Lily answered and (with

her typical sassy scowl) said, "Wassup, delivery boy?"

"Your cat tore up our apartment, that's what's up!"

Lily gave him a smirk. "Oh, really."

"Yes, really!" Dave said, then grabbed her by the arm and pulled her along.

Now, Dave was never commanding or demanding (or even firm) with Lily. And this change in him was so surprising to Lily that she simply let him drag her next door.

"See?" he said, pointing at the scratched wall.

Lily, however, didn't look at the wall. Instead, she took in the topsy-turvy state of things. "Nice housekeeping," she said.

"Thanks to your *cat*," Dave snapped. He moved across the room and pointed above his head to the gouges in the ceiling. "See those? Your cat is a monster!"

Lily looked around. "You think a *cat* did this?" She laughed. "You're funny, delivery boy."

Dave started throwing cushions back onto the sofa and chairs. "She came in through the kitchen window, she tore around after my pet lizard—"

"Oh, so now you're admitting it's your pet?"

"Look," Dave snapped, "it comes in and out, okay? It's, you know, a good-luck charm."

She sniggered as she looked around. "I can see how *that's* workin' for ya."

"The lizard's not the problem, your cat is! She's possessed!"

"Oh, *really?*" Lily said, then hurried out of the apartment, only to return a minute later with one very droopy-looking Topaz. "You think this cat is possessed? You think she tore through your house and gouged up your *ceiling?*"

Topaz did seem like nothing more than a help-less, hapless furry blob. (One that might have a propensity for ramming walls with her face, but catapulting eight feet to sink her claws into a ceiling? Not likely.)

Still, Dave held his ground. "Yes!"

Dave and Lily locked eyes for a moment. "Well," Lily said (in her sassy, saucy way), "you're crazy." She eyed the ceiling. "There's no way *any* cat can get up that high." She shrugged. "Besides, Topaz has been sacked out since I got home."

"Oh yeah?" Dave challenged, but something about what she'd said gave him pause. "Uh, when *did* you get home?"

She shrugged again. "A while ago."

Dave simply stood there, thinking and blinking.

Now, the truth was that Lily had not been home that long, but she'd been home long enough to blow Sticky's story wide open. And after she left with a "See ya, delivery dork," Dave took a deep breath and said, "Stickyyyyyyy?"

The little gecko peeked out from his hiding place inside Dave's sweatshirt and looked at Dave with extreme innocence. *"Sí, señor?"* But as Dave studied him, the lying gecko started to feel the heat.

His eyes went a little shifty.

His face went a little twitchy.

And as Dave's eyes narrowed, Sticky knew he was busted.

"Ay-ay-ay," Sticky moaned. "I gave that evil *gata* some of the potion, okay?"

Dave's eyes flew open. "You WHAT?"

"It was just a drop. How was I supposed to know it would make her as strong as an ox?"

"That's the whole point!" Dave shouted. "You didn't know! What if it had *killed* her?"

Sticky looked off to the side and gave a little shrug.

"Sticky!"

"Hey! She's been trying to kill *me* for weeks and you didn't care about that!"

"So you *were* trying to kill her?"

"No!"

Dave spittered and spattered and sputtered until at last he gave up trying to figure out what to say to Sticky and got busy putting the family room in order.

When he'd done as much as he could, his head

was at least clear enough to form a question. "So," he asked, "where's the potion?"

"Ay-ay-ay," Sticky replied.

Dave stopped in his tracks. "What? Where is it? What happened to it?"

And so the story came out about the monkey and the potion and Sticky's efforts to recover the powerful liquid. "I tried, *señor*, but that monkey was jumping all over the place, throwing things around. . . . You should see your room! And he stole your grill!"

"I don't care about that stupid grill!" Dave snapped as he hurried toward his room. "It wasn't even mine! *You* stole it from someone else!"

And then Dave saw his room.

"I can't *believe* this!" he wailed.

But as he staggered through the mess, the thing that dealt the final blow was his social studies project.

It was, without question, destroyed.

(It was also, without exception, due the next day.)

And between the missing potion, the chaos throughout the house, and the lies (and yes, the mutilated school project), Dave had had enough. "You quit going to school with me, you hang out with criminals, you steal stuff, and you give cats potions that could kill them. Plus, you made me look like a total *idiot* in front of Lily!" He shook his head. "That's it. I used to think you were a good gecko with a bad habit, but I was wrong."

He opened his bedroom window and placed Sticky on the wall outside. "Enough is enough." And with that, he closed the window, shutting Sticky out of the apartment.

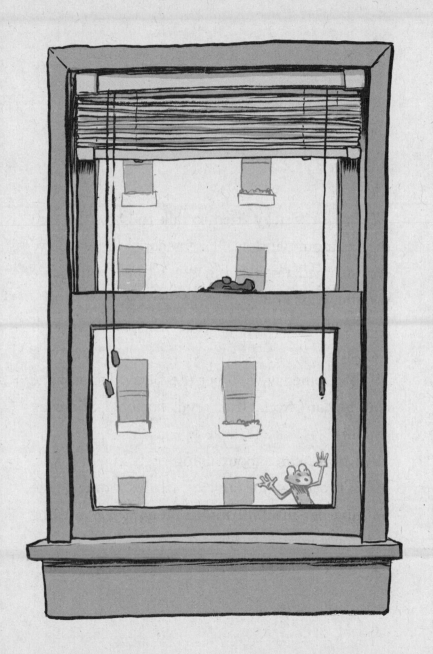

Chapter 14
SHUT OUT

That night, Sticky tried to talk to Dave through the bedroom window. "Psst, *señor*! I know you're one steamed tamale, but don't forget who gave you the wristband."

"Leave me alone!" Dave whispered through the pane.

"But someday we'll get the Buzzy Bee and the Half-a-Man from that evil *hombre*. Someday you'll—"

"I don't care about flying or being invisible. I don't care about any of it! It's brought me nothing but trouble. *You've* brought me nothing but trouble!"

"You cut me to the quick, *señor*!" Sticky cried,

and this time there was only hurt in the little gecko's voice.

Dave sighed and dropped the blinds. "Just go away!"

It was at this point that Dave's mother entered his room. "*Mi'jo?* Are you all right?" she asked.

"Uh . . . yeah," Dave replied. "I'm just, uh, practicing my lines for drama."

Mrs. Sanchez was concerned (as Dave had acted anxious throughout dinner and, despite his explanation, seemed very keyed up now). But she didn't press him. He was, after all, thirteen, and she remembered all too well what that was like. Instead, she simply said, "Let me know if there's anything I can help you with." She looked around the room, which was still quite messy. "This weekend, let's get this cleaned up, okay, *mi'jo?*"

Dave nodded, wondering what his parents would do when they finally noticed the damage to the family room wall and ceiling.

However, whether because of their exhaustion or having to deal with more pressing matters (like paying bills), they didn't seem to see it. And as evening turned into night, then ticked toward bedtime and beyond, Dave's frayed nerves seemed to weave themselves back together. At midnight, he declared his social studies project to be done enough and went to bed.

As Dave drifted off to sleep, he did have a brief relapse of panic over the missing potion, but he pushed it aside. What did it matter? If the monkey had it, he wouldn't actually *eat* it. It smelled terrible! And if anyone found it, they would take one whiff and throw it away.

No, instead of worrying about the potion, he thought about what a relief it was that he was done being the Gecko. He took off the powerband and hid it under his pillow. He hadn't gotten to do anything *super* with it, anyway. Not really. All it had done was attract the wrath of Damien Black.

So, despite the traumas of the day, Dave slept well, and after the usual morning rush, he headed off to school, balancing his project on his bike.

That same night, however, Sticky did not sleep a wink.

He knew that the things Dave had said were true, and he felt terrible. And as he clung to Dave's bedroom window hoping that Dave would have a change of heart, he wondered what in the world he could do to make it up to Dave.

How could he get him to forgive him?

How could he prove that he *was* a good gecko?

How could he convince Dave that he couldn't quit being the Gecko? Didn't he know that Damien Black was a menace not just to them but to everyone in the city? Didn't he know by now that Damien Black wasn't someone you could turn your back on?

That doing so would mean death?

Despite the trouble Sticky had caused, they had intercepted a potion that Damien was planning to use for . . . well, Sticky didn't know, exactly . . . but it was undoubtedly evil. And keeping it from Damien was a good thing! *They* were a good thing, and Sticky was part of that "they."

By sunrise Sticky had convinced himself that there was one sure way to get Dave to both forgive him *and* want to be the Gecko again.

It meant going up to Damien Black's monstrous mansion.

It meant risking his life.

Still. Being caught and captured (or killed) was better than this.

Anything was better than this.

And so it was that Sticky began the long journey up to Raven Ridge.

This time, alone.

Chapter 15
THINGS THAT GO BWA-HA-CAW IN THE NIGHT

While Sticky was clinging to the wall outside Dave's room and Dave was inside sleeping soundly, the Bandito Brothers were also outside, shivering and quivering in the dark and dangerous forest.

I'm sure you've heard of "circling the wagons." This is something the American pioneers did with their covered wagons for protection against attack in the wild western plains and to corral their livestock when setting up camp.

They weren't, however, the first to do this. Gypsies, too, circled their vardos for protection, shelter, and community as they traveled across foreign (and often hostile) lands.

Unfortunately for the Bandito Brothers, they had no wagons—covered, vardo, or otherwise.

(Well, Tito did, back home, but it was a little red one, so never mind.)

And having no wagons to circle, the Brothers circled themselves instead. They sat face out, leaning their backs against the trunk of a large, gnarled pine tree, remaining wide-eyed as they shivered through the snarls and moans, howls and groans of the long, dark night.

At last, daybreak arrived. (It was, in fact, close to noon, but because of the dark density of that part of the forest, the sun was only able to break through when it was almost directly overhead.)

The forest was still full of frightening sounds, but instead of snarls and moans, howls and groans, the Brothers now heard rustling.

Rustling that seemed to be coming from every direction.

"Wolves!" Angelo gasped. "I think we're surrounded by wolves!"

Pablo, being both smaller and rattier than the hairy-armed Angelo, hid behind the second Brother, thinking that there was plenty enough Angelo for a whole pack of wolves.

But Tito had his simple mind on something more pressing than a potential pack of wolves.

He really, really, really needed to find some toilet paper.

"HELP!" he shouted into the air. "WE'RE LOST! HELP!"

Before the other two Brothers could tell him how stupid he was, there was a response from overhead.

"Bwa-ha-caw! Bwa-ha-caw!"

"Boss?" Pablo asked, his ratty face darting around.

"Bwa-ha-caw!" came the response, only this time it was a loud, dissonant chorus of bwa-ha-cawing.

"Aaaah!" Angelo cried, covering his ears against the nightmare of hideous laughter.

Suddenly the Brothers were surrounded by ravens.

(Or, more accurately, oversized crows.)

"Aaaaah!" Pablo cried (and again, he cowered behind Angelo).

Tito, however, was *really* desperate now and simply shouted, "I NEED A POTTY!" as he charged through the forest.

Apparently, the bwa-ha-cawing crows wanted the Brothers out of their forest as much as the Brothers wanted to get out, because the crows chased after them, guiding the Brothers along with angry pecks and bwa-ha-cawing head swooshes.

The Brothers crashed and thundered through the forest for what seemed like an eternity, and just as Tito was thinking he would never, ever make it, the trees thinned and the mansion appeared ahead.

"I've got dibs on the potty!" Tito cried, and

charged into the house and straight for the bathroom.

Unfortunately, someone else had been skipping to the loo all night, and the only nearby facility was currently occupied.

"Where have you bozos been?" Damien shouted through the bathroom door.

"Lost!" Tito cried, then squirmed and squiggled and held tight to his gut. "Mr. Black! I've really got to GO!"

"Use the one in your quarters!" the angry treasure hunter shouted back.

"I'll never make it!" Tito wailed. "Please, Mr. Black. I'M GONNA EXPLODE!"

Perhaps Damien Black took pity on the poor Brother.

Perhaps he felt his pain.

Or, more likely, he was about done anyway.

But *most* likely, Damien didn't want an explosion (of any sort, but especially not of *that* sort) in

his house. So, with uncharacteristic acquiescence, he whooshed open the door and allowed Tito access to his (extremely pee-yoo'd) loo.

Meanwhile, the other Brothers had also arrived, and Damien wasted no time in tearing into them. "You block-headed bozos! You knuckleheaded ninnies! You idiotic, incompetent imbeciles! Where have you been?"

"Trapped in the forest, boss!" Pablo said. "We barely escaped with our lives!"

"You're telling me you don't have the monkey *or* the coffee?"

Angelo and Pablo shook their sorry heads.

"You dim-witted dummies!" Damien shouted. "You slug-brained sloths! You . . . you chowderheaded chumps!"

With each insult, Damien's usually pallid face grew redder. The ends of his twisty mustache quivered and shivered. Steam seemed to shoot from his ears. And just as it appeared that Damien

Black would be the thing exploding, he suddenly took a deep breath, closed his eyes, and said, "You . . . *owe* . . . me."

"Anything, boss. We'll do anything!" Pablo said in his jumpy, ratty way.

Damien's left eye cocked open. His other eye stayed slitty and sly.

Slowly, a sneer arched up his face and he began twisting his mustache. "Yessss," he hissed. "I would say you will."

Another diabolical deal had just been sealed.

Chapter 16
STICKY GETS THE SHAFT

It took Sticky all day to get up to Raven Ridge.

It is, after all, quite a distance (with a lot of uphill).

Not that he walked.

Oh no.

He stowed away, zippy-toeing from one vehicle to another, zigging and zagging his way through the city. It was, as I'm sure you might imagine, a very inefficient way to get someplace. Still, it was better than walking, and with a little persistence, he (at last) found himself on a car that zoomed him up the road to Raven Ridge.

(Of course, he had to dive into a bush when the car crested the ridge, because nobody stops there unless they have to, but this wasn't the first time Sticky had launched himself like a little gecko rocket, and he landed just fine.)

Now, as you may have already figured out, Sticky's mission in going to the mansion was to get his hands on the remaining powerband ingots.

Or, at least, as many as he could escape with.

Specifically Flying.

How could Dave still be mad at him if he delivered the Flying ingot?

How could Dave not want to be the Gecko again?

And so it was that Sticky risked life and limb to get up to Raven Ridge, traverse the fearsome forest, enter the maniacal mansion, and work his way down, down, down to the deep, dark (and frightfully stinky) depths of Damien's dungeon. A dungeon that housed, among other torturous terrors, the deadly Komodo dragon that protected

Damien's vast treasure trove of ill-gotten gold and jewels and priceless artwork.

Or, at least, it used to.

To Sticky's dismay, all that remained in the dragon's den was . . . the dragon.

"Ay *caramba*, no!" he moaned.

Now, Damien Black may be despicable and demented, dastardly and deadly, but anyone would agree: He's no dummy.

And knowing (as he did) that he'd been infiltrated by Dave and Sticky once, and thinking (as he did) that they might call the cops on him (or worse, the IRS), he knew he had to find a new place to store his treasures. He could not, however, see hauling things up the way he'd brought them down—via long, dark flights of steep, narrow steps. That may have been fine for taking pieces in one by one, over time, but now he wanted to get them out all at once, and quickly.

And so it was that after some complex calculations, Damien had punctured the floor of a little-used west-wing room and, with an auger, bored a shaft that went down, down, down into soil, grit, and granite (and an elaborate network of gopher tunnels), until it broke through the top of the dragon's den.

Then, bucket by bucket, he'd simply (or, in the case of two life-sized statues, not so simply) hoisted the treasures up, up, up and stashed them in various secure and secluded (and, at times, sinister) places around the mansion.

Now, of all the priceless artifacts and precious jewelry and pricey Ming pottery, Damien's most treasured possessions were the four remaining power ingots.

Strength, Speed, Invisibility, and Flying.

(He didn't give two beans about Wall-Walker. The one small comfort he found in the whole powerband situation was that at least the pint-sized punk who had it couldn't do much with it.)

And so, because the remaining power ingots were the most prized of all his possessions, he had hidden them around the mansion in locations so sneaky and creepy that no pesky little thief, no rotten little robber, no brazen little boy would even dare approach them!

Unfortunately for Damien, Sticky had been his prisoner and knew how Damien's dastardly (and decidedly demented) mind worked.

Sticky had also witnessed Damien's use of one of these four spots for concealing a pilfered 1728 Spanish gold doubloon (which, although not worth as much as one might think, was treasured by Damien because it made him feel so . . . piratey).

So, as fate would have it, of all the sneaky, creepy, not-supposed-to-peeky places in the whole monstrous mansion, this was, in fact, the *first* place Sticky thought to look.

It was also the very last place he would ever want to be.

But he was on a mission.

A mission to restore Dave's faith in him.

A mission to bring the Gecko back.

And so it was that Sticky steeled himself against the fear of what he was about to face and started up the shaft that would take him to the west wing of the mansion.

It was, you see, where Damien kept the tarantula tank.

Chapter 17
A TERRIFYING TANK OF TARANTULAS

It's a well-known fact that tarantulas are both hairy and scary. What you may not know, however, is that tarantulas range in size from only about one inch to over ten.

Oh.

And that they are carnivorous.

Now, what sort of meat do you suppose a ten-inch spider eats?

Let me give you a little hint.

The ten-inch species of tarantulas may be known among scientists as *Theraphosa blondi*, but explorers who first discovered it in the rain forests of South America named it the Goliath bird eater.

That's right.

It's a spider that eats birds.

But . . . how in the world does a spider *catch* a bird?

Not with a sumo-sized web.

Oh no.

Unlike other spiders, tarantulas do not spin webs.

They hunt.

At night.

Like eight-legged, furry-fanged cats.

Yes, a tarantula stalks its prey, slowly creeps up on it, and then pounces, grasping tight with its re-tractable claws. Then (unlike a cat) it sinks its furry fangs into its victim, pumps it with venom, and (through a process involving regurgitation) turns the prey's innards into a slurpy stew.

(Yum, huh?)

Tarantulas, for the record, are also cannibalistic.

Now, in case there's any confusion, "cannibalistic" does not mean that they like to do cannonballs into rivers or streams (or, for that matter, their water dish, should they be in captivity).

They actually (and factually) hate water (except, that is, for drinking).

No, by "cannibalistic," I mean that they will eat their own kind.

Soupify their hairy, scary neighbor.

Feast on the fangy fiend confined to the same cage.

Yes, disturbing as it may be, it is, in fact, a spider-slurp-spider world, something Damien Black learned the hard way, losing several dozen Goliath bird eaters before figuring it out.

Not one to concede defeat, Damien switched to an aggressive, burrowing species, velvety brown in color and about the size of an adult hand. They were easier to maintain, and he solved (for the most part) the cannibalism problem by automating the spiders' food supply, introducing grasshoppers once a week via a hopper that fed in through the fifty-gallon terrarium's mesh lid.

Now, because Damien Black is demented and dastardly (and dare I say . . . different?), he outfitted his tarantula terrarium like a desert island. And although the three feet of subsoil was suitable for burrowing, the top layer was sand.

With (real) driftwood.

And (little fake) palm trees.

And (little fake) seagulls.

And a (little fake) Jolly Roger flag.

And a (little fake) ocean (which doubled as a water dish).

And buried beneath the sand (in a very sly location) was a (little fake) pirate chest.

It was inside this pirate chest that Damien kept his (very real) 1728 Spanish gold doubloon. *And,* Sticky suspected, the powerband's other ingots.

It just made sense.

(In a decidedly demented Damien Black sort of way.)

And so it was that Sticky went up the dragon den shaft and into the mansion's west wing and zippy-toed through cobwebbed corridors, past the bone room, past the spear room, past the creepy candelabra room, along the wall of a booby-trapped set of stairs, and down a final dark and dingy corridor, until at last he reached the spider room.

The tarantula terrarium was located near a bookcase. There were, in fact, a lot of books in the room, and if it hadn't been for the storage of odd-sized cages and terrariums (and the grasshopper hopper coming down through the ceiling), the room would have seemed more like a study than a spider room.

Inside the terrarium, three velvety spiders were visible, resting beneath broad pieces of driftwood in far corners of the enclosure, but there were, in fact, many (*many*) more that had retreated into the cool darkness of their burrows.

Sticky's little heart started racing.

These tarantulas, you see, while not bird killers, did enjoy a variety of food. Grasshoppers (obviously), but also crickets and frogs and, yes, lizards.

And Damien had, at one wicked point in his control over Sticky, placed him in the tarantula tank.

Not to feed his hairy, scary monsters.

Oh no.

He had done it to make Sticky talk.

You see, after Sticky discovered that Damien was nothing more than a dirty double-crosser, he'd simply stopped speaking to him (a tactic you yourself have probably employed at least once).

To counteract this, Damien did not try reasoning with the gecko.

Nor did he put him in time-out (as Sticky was already confined to a cage, which is, in essence, a permanent time-out).

He also didn't implore him to just grow up.

No, he simply tossed him in the tank.

And after being stalked and chased by an army of hungry tarantulas, after scaling the walls to escape only to be swatted down again and again by Damien, after holding out for as long as lizardly possible, Sticky finally cried, "All right, all right! I'll talk!"

A smug, sinister smile had crossed Damien's face as he'd snatched the poor gecko up to safety and promptly re-caged him.

So! It's no wonder Sticky's heart was *ka-pow-pow-powing* in his chest as he climbed up the terrarium.

It's no wonder he was shaky-toed and light-headed as he stood on the mesh lid of the terrarium and peered down at the fierce, furry monsters below.

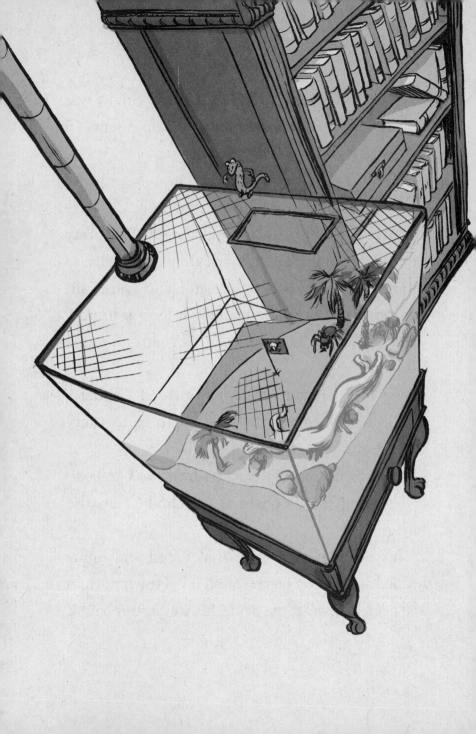

It's also no wonder that he thought (for more than a moment) that he was *loco*-berry burritos and should forget the whole idea.

But Sticky really is a good and (despite evidence to the contrary) honorable gecko, and in the end he decided it was worth the risk.

He took a deep, steadying breath.

He verrrrry carefully opened the mesh window in the terrarium's top.

And then the gutsy gecko, summoning every ounce of his courage, stepped inside.

Chapter 18
INSIDE THE PIRATE CHEST

Tarantulas (like many spiders) have eight eyes, but their eyesight is weak. Instead, they rely on sensory hairs that can feel even the slightest vibrations on the ground or in the air.

It was, therefore, futile for Sticky to sneaky-toe down to the (fake) desert island, but charging down would also have been a mistake, as sudden movements make tarantulas feel threatened, and a tarantula that feels threatened defends itself by shooting off venomous body hairs.

Having had some experience with this the last time he was in the tank, Sticky decided to err on the side of caution, and moved along the inside rim of the enclosure as smoothly and silently as possible.

Still. Perhaps it was the vibrations he caused as he walked along the glass.

Or perhaps it was the manic beating of his heart.

Or the fact that the grasshopper hopper hadn't dropped anything to eat in over a week.

Regardless, by the time Sticky was above a small grove of (little fake) palm trees, spiders were beginning to emerge from their burrows.

"*Ay caramba!*" Sticky gasped (causing more vibrations to move through the air).

He clung to the glass a moment, watching as hairy legs emerged from underground. Then, realizing that the situation was not improving over time, he made a mad dash for the mound of sand in front of the (little fake) palm trees and began digging furiously.

As he dug, spiders approached.

Cautiously.

Tarantulas are, for the record, speedy runners,

but these were in the presence of other (cannibalistic) spiders and were a little uncertain as to how to negotiate this meal.

"*Ay chihuahua!*" Sticky cried (because the hairy monsters were approaching plenty fast enough for him!).

To ward them off, Sticky turned around and dug like a dog, spraying sand in their eight-eyed faces. This, of course, ticked off the tarantulas, causing some of them to rise up on their back legs and produce a hissing sound while showing their fangs.

"Holy moly tacarole!" Sticky whimpered (as he peered at them between his legs).

The situation was, in fact, so dire that Sticky had no time to open the treasure chest, even though he'd reached it. Instead, he escaped the hissing herd of hairy beasties by zippy-toeing around the (little fake) palm trees and scampering into the (little fake) ocean. "Get back, you freaky *fieras!*" he cried, and began scooping water at them.

Well! If you're ever on a desert island (little fake or otherwise) and you're being attacked by a hungry herd of tarantulas, just spray them with water. They will retreat, and you will find your uncovered treasure chest (at least temporarily) unguarded.

Sticky could not believe his luck and wasted no time in getting back to the chest.

His heart was clacking like castanets as he pulled open the lid.

His hopes were sky-high.

But as he peered inside the chest, he discovered that it held only one item:

The 1728 Spanish gold doubloon.

"*Ay caramba,* no!" Sticky cried, for regardless of how cool and shiny a 1728 Spanish gold doubloon might be, it was not worth facing hairy, scary spiders to get to.

But then he noticed a glow coming from around the inside edges of the treasure chest lid.

There was a panel across the lid, and when he released it, he found himself face to face with a single notched coin.

One that glowed brighter than any doubloon.

One that shimmered like a pool of sunshine.

One that had designs on it that were both foreign and mysterious.

It was a single, solitary power ingot, but oh, what a power ingot!

"The Buzzy Bee!" Sticky cried, snatching it up.

Right behind him, however, a hungry tarantula was preparing to pounce.

"*Ay caramba!*" Sticky cried, and did a three-legged dart away from the beast, leaping over another to get onto the glass side of the terrarium.

All the spiders suddenly wanted in on the action, clamoring and climbing and (yes) clawing to get over one another to the lizard.

But before they could reach him, Sticky
clamped the ingot in his mouth and zippy-toed
up the glass wall, across the mesh covering, and
out the mesh window, escaping the terrifying tank
of tarantulas.

Unfortunately, before Sticky could spend even a moment catching his breath, he heard a sound more terrifying than the hiss of tarantulas.

More frightening than the threat of fierce and fuzzy fangs.

More horrific than a stampeding herd of hairy, scary spiders.

It was the bone-chilling, heart-stopping, knee-knocking voice of Damien Black.

Chapter 19
THE INNER SANCTUM

Sticky had no time to think, so he simply reacted. He dived from the terrarium lid to the bookcase, then turbo-toed inside a little tepee formed by a wooden box and a book.

"You boneheaded bozos!" came Damien's voice as he blasted into the room. "You meatheaded morons! You chowder-brained chumps! I can't believe I'm having to do all this because you can't read!"

"Sorry, boss!" came Pablo's crackly voice.

Now, as you may have already deduced, the Bandito Brothers were not trailing along behind Damien.

They (and their bucktoothed burro, Rosie)

were waiting for him outside the mansion, near the bat cave (which was, in fact, a cave full of bats, as opposed to, say, *another* bat cave that might spring to mind). Damien Black was simply multi-tasking, retrieving some last-minute supplies as he continued his conversation with the Brothers through his walkie-talkie communicator. (The communicator was another Damien contraption, and it had, among other things, a long, spirally antenna, a grid-shaped doohickey, a fan-shaped thingamabob, lots of copper wires, glowing tubes, and *lips*.)

It was because Damien was preoccupied with the communicator (and was in a frothy fury over the Brothers) that he stormed right past the (open) pirate chest and the (open) tarantula terrarium and (without even glancing over his shoulder) revealed the secret entry to his innermost sanctum.

Not even Sticky knew of this cloak-and-dagger passageway or the secret room to which it led. The room was so hush-hush, in fact, that no one (and I mean no one) had ever been inside it.

(Well, except for the ruthless villain himself, of course.)

Granted, this was most likely due to visitors being a rare (and unwanted) thing at the Black mansion, because the cloak-and-dagger passageway was actually quite ordinary.

Curiously conventional.

Something any mystery reader would immediately point to and say, "Ah-ha! Secret passageway!"

Still. Like so many things in the mansion, it was something Damien took childish delight in having. So (despite his frothy fury) it was with a great and satisfying *whoosh-swoosh* that he pushed through a revolving bookcase.

A revolving bookcase that happened to have Sticky on board.

Well! Sticky was most certainly thinking, "Holy guacamole!" but (for once) he managed to keep his little lizard lips zipped.

(Well, as zipped as lips can be with a power ingot still clamped between them.)

He held his breath and watched (with one sneaky-peeky eye) as Damien flicked on a light. (Something that was quite necessary, as there were no windows whatsoever in this inner sanctum.)

Next, Damien slammed and bammed doors and drawers, stuffing items into the deep, dark pockets of his long black coat. And then, quite suddenly, he stopped slamming and bamming and held completely still.

It was as though he'd heard something.

Smelled something.

Sensed something.

Slowly, he turned toward the bookcase, his eyes dark, narrow slits, the pointy points of his mustache twitching.

A devilish sneer smeared his face.

But just as Sticky was about to shake into a thousand gecko pieces, Damien swooped down on his heavily carved (and astonishingly detailed) desk and snatched up the funkydoodle phone.

One long, pointy finger pressed into a fossilized shark vertebra and dialed.

Swish, click-click-click-click.

Swish, click-click-click-click-clack!

Damien dialed the number (which took some time, as the funkydoodle dial was, well, funkydoodle).

Then Damien waited.

One ringy-dingy.

Two.

His left eyebrow was arched high.

His right was crouched low, as if ready to pounce.

And then, out of the cheesy speaker, Sticky could hear, "*Sastimos.*"

"*Sastimos*" is, in case you're not already familiar, a Romany greeting. Its basic translation is "to your health," but it can be used like "hello."

This word—this single word—caused a demented smile to cross Damien's already dastardly face.

He did not say hello in return.

(Or, for that matter, wish the person on the other end good health.)

Instead, he (very quietly) put the receiver down and muttered, "Double-dealing gypsy! You think you can pull a fast one on *me*? Well, I'm on my way to teach you a lesson!" His expression dropped to a mere scowl. "I should bring backup," he muttered, "in case those buffoons botch things up."

He turned, and suddenly (with another *whoosh-swoosh*) he was in front of the bookcase.

Sticky choked back an "Ay-ay-ay!" as Damien's hand shot straight for the wooden-box part of his tepee and yanked it from the shelf. The remaining book fell on Sticky, but as Damien whoosh-swooshed back to his desk, Sticky managed to pull himself to a new (and less painful) hiding place in time to see Damien snap open the wooden box.

The box held a matching pair of percussion-lock dueling pistols (along with a powder flask, rods for cleaning and loading, percussion caps, and a bullet mold).

It was a rare and valuable (not to mention stunning) set of weapons, with gilded muzzles, side plates, and hammers, and the grips were so beautifully carved that the guns looked more like swanky pirate movie props than actual weapons.

They were, however, the real deal.

They shot large, bone-shattering bullets.

Little cannonballs, really.

And although each pistol could fire but one bullet at a time, the guns were highly accurate and had outstanding muzzle velocity and (most

importantly) smooth bores, which made the bullets they fired untraceable.

And they were so much more spiffidy-doo-dah than modern handguns that their size and limitations were, to Damien's mind, not an issue.

He was, after all, a deadly and merciless shot.

Damien lifted both pistols from their box, then hesitated. One had always sufficed in the past, and he did have a lot of other things to manage.

But there was something about wearing a brace of pistols that made him feel fully loaded.

Fueled for duel.

So Damien cut the moment of hesitation short and proceeded to load and holster both pistols. And then, with another dramatic *whoosh-swoosh*, Damien clicked off the light and exited his inner sanctum through a *second* revolving bookcase, leaving Sticky trapped inside.

Chapter 20
TRAPPED!

Clicking the light back on was not a problem for Sticky.

Admitting he was trapped inside was.

But there were no windows, no vents, no chimney or visible ductwork . . . and the revolving bookcases were much too heavy for him to push.

"Freaky *frijoles*. Are you serious, man?" he muttered. "I've got the Buzzy Bee! I've got to get out of here!"

Unfortunately, the Flying ingot (or, if you prefer, the Buzzy Bee) was of no use to Sticky. It was useless without the powerband, and the powerband was useless on Sticky. (Not only was it way too big, but it only seemed to work on humans.)

Besides, what good would flying around a room do?

There was still no way out.

"If only I had the potion," Sticky grumbled, "I could push through the turning books and *vámonos!*"

Sticky may not have had the Moongaze potion, but there *was* a funkydoodle phone. He didn't like the looks of it (as a bird claw, taxidermied or not, is a fierce and frightening thing to any lizard), but after realizing he was most definitely trapped, he climbed up Damien's devilishly carved desk and approached the contraption.

The Sanchezes, of course, had a phone in their apartment.

A regular, plastic, push-button model.

And (having lived inside the apartment awhile now, and having heard it repeated enough) Sticky did know the Sanchezes' phone number.

And (after witnessing Damien's use of it) he

recognized that this funkydoodle contraption on the villain's desk was, indeed, a telephone.

One that needed to be dialed.

And so it was that Sticky wrestled the receiver off the cradle and began making his first phone call.

It was a difficult process.

One full of flubs and blubs and boo-boos.

Time and again the dial got away from him, and time and again he had to start over. It was, indeed, a difficult process, but with each bobble, Sticky grew more determined.

He had to get the Buzzy Bee to Dave.

He just had to!

Meanwhile, Dave (who was done with his afternoon deliveries) was coming home to an empty house.

Now, by "empty," I do not mean that all the furniture and dishes and appliances had been stolen.

By "empty," I mean lonely.

There was no "Hey, *señooooor!*"

No "*Excelente picante!* You're home!"

No "I'm out here, *señor!* Having a sizzly *siesta.*"

Just quiet.

Sad, lonely quiet.

Dave parked his bike, dumped his backpack, and heaved a sigh. It had been a day even rougher than most. This was due, in part, to the sneers and jeers (and kitty-cat jokes) made by Lily and her sassy, saucy friends. But it was also because Dave now realized that his old friends had somehow drifted away. Regrouped. Left the kid with the strange habit of talking to himself behind.

Not that Dave was actually talking to *himself.* He'd been talking to Sticky.

Worrying about the powerband.

Obsessing over Damien Black.

But today, as he'd made a real effort to reconnect with some old friends, he'd discovered that they weren't interested in reconnecting with him. Over the past few months, he'd become known as a dorky dude with spastic behaviors.

Someone to avoid.

So it was with a heavy heart that Dave returned home, and finding that Sticky had gone away (just as he'd commanded) made him even sadder.

When the telephone rang, Dave almost didn't answer it.

Why bother?

It was probably his mother or father wanting him to do some errand.

But the phone continued to ring, and when Dave at last checked caller ID, he was puzzled.

The readout was blank.

Finally he punched the ON button and said a tentative "Hello?"

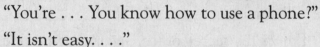

"*Señor!* Is it you?"

Dave did some rapid-fire blinking. "Sticky?"

"*Híjole!* It *is* you!"

"You're . . . You know how to use a phone?"

"It isn't easy. . . ."

This, as you know, was an understatement. Sticky now had the funkydoodle phone on its side and was speaking into the ivory horn, then turning his head to hear what was snap-crackle-popping out of the cheesy speaker.

"Where are you?" Dave asked.

"Ay-ay-ay. You don't want to know. But I have good news!"

"You're at that madman's mansion, aren't you?" Dave said, thinking way ahead of any possible good news.

"*Sí, señor*, but that's the bad news."

"Are you hurt? Why did you go there?"

"I'm fine, *señor*. Although I did almost get munchy-crunched by big, ugly spiders."

"What?"

"Never mind. The bad news is I'm trapped."

"Trapped? Did Damien catch you? Where are you? I'll come get you."

"I'm in his secret office, *señor*, but he doesn't know it. I sneaky-toed up the dragon chimney—"

"Wait. The dragon has a chimney?"

"*Sí, señor*. It's new. It goes up to a room next to a hall with spidery clouds—"

"Spidery clouds?" Dave racked his brains. "You mean cobwebs?"

"*Sí!* That's what you call them. You go by a room with big white bones, and one with big, pointy knives on sticks, and one with big-handed candleholders, and then up some stairs. . . . They're booby-trapped, though, so you have to use Gecko Power and go along the wall." Sticky was quiet for a split second, then said, "Wear the powerband, okay, *señor*? We're going to need it to help the potion man."

"Wait. What's he got to do with this?"

Sticky made a little clicking sound. "That evil *hombre* thinks he's a dirty double-crosser."

Dave gasped. "Because of the potion?"

"*Sí, señor*. I think so."

Dave stood in his kitchen, stunned. Why hadn't he thought this might happen? "This is all my fault!" he cried.

"It's my fault, too, *señor*. I'm sorry."

"Do you know what Damien's going to do?"

"No, *señor*, but it has something to do with Pablo and Angelo. And he took two *pistolas*."

"Guns?"

"*Sí*. But they're not six-shooters." Sticky tried to shake off the memory of having seen them in action before. "They're only one-shooters."

"They're still guns!"

"But I have something that will help us stop him. You just have to get me out of here!"

Dave was thinking too fast to really hear what Sticky was saying. So instead of asking what Sticky had that would help them, he said, "But how am I ever going to find you? That place is crazy, and there are booby traps everywhere! And I can't get in through the Komodo dragon den— that monster will rip me to shreds!"

"Hmm," Sticky said, and Dave could practically see him tapping his little gecko chin. "That *loco lobo* is gone, so just picture where the dragon cave is and climb in a window above it."

"But . . . I don't even know if I know where it is! It was all twists and turns when we went down before."

"Oh, you can do it, *señor*. And once you're inside, just walk around until you find the spider room."

"The spider room?"

"*Sí, señor.* It has a big glass cage with giant, hairy spiders in it."

"Oh, great," Dave said (his voice sounding rather squeaky).

"When you're in the spider room, push on the bookcase. It spins like a merry-go-round. I'm in the secret room on the other side."

"But . . . what if I can't find it?"

"Then I'll have to find some other way to give you the Buzzy Bee."

"The Buzzy . . . ? You found it? You've got Flying?"

"*Sí, señor.* And it was pretty hairy-scary."

Dave understood immediately why Sticky had gone to the mansion. And he knew from experience that Sticky had risked life and limb to do this for him. "Aw, Sticky . . ."

"Just *ándale*, okay, *hombre*? Put on the powerband and let's go help the potion man."

A strange feeling came over Dave.

One of strength.

Determination.

Sticky *was* his friend.

From now on, nothing was going to change that.

Dave nodded. "Hold on, little buddy. I'm on my way."

Chapter 21
TRAIL OF TARANTULAS

Damien Black's mansion was so devilishly devised, so curiously convoluted, so horribly hodgepodged that it was, in fact, highly unlikely that Dave would ever find Sticky.

Except for one small detail.

A trail.

Now, this trail was not made of bread crumbs.

Oh no.

It was a trail of hairy, scary spiders fleeing the mansion through an opening in a second-story window.

"Holy smokes!" Dave gasped when he noticed the spiders. "He wasn't joking!"

Dave was in his Gecko getup—sunglasses, a

ball cap (a bandanna at the ready), a plain black T-shirt, and jeans. Under his shirtsleeve, the Wall-Walker ingot was clicked inside the powerband.

Dave watched the spiders a moment, then scaled the wall, avoiding the hairy beasts as he climbed in through the open window.

Once inside, Dave simply moved against the stream of tarantulas. (It was a sparse stream, but speedy. And each time Dave thought he had run out of mad-dashing spiders, another one appeared, racing along the cobwebby corridor to

catch up to the spider that had gotten away before it.)

"The bone room!" Dave laughed when he came upon it. "I found the bone room!"

(Never mind that there were real, fully formed skeletons on stands—Dave was just happy to be on the right path.)

From there, it was easy. He passed by the spear room and the creepy candelabra room. He remembered to take the wall, bypassing the booby-trapped stairs, and then he hurried down the dark and dingy (and now also creepy-crawly) corridor until at last he reached the spider room.

"Sticky!" he cried as he pushed through the revolving bookcase.

Sticky quickly slapped down the disconnect lever on the funkydoodle phone. *"Señor!"*

Despite how happy Dave was to see Sticky (and vice versa), he noticed that there was something fishy about Sticky's reaction.

"What *is* that?" Dave asked, pointing to the funkydoodle phone.

"Uh . . . it's that evil *hombre*'s ring-a-ling?"

Dave eyed him suspiciously. "Why do you look so guilty?"

Sticky's eyes shifted to the left.

They shifted to the right.

Suddenly *Dave's* eyes popped wide. "You were making crank calls?"

Sticky gave a little gecko shrug. "I was bored, *señor.*"

But then, lickety-split, the naughty lizard zippy-toed to a hiding place behind the desk and produced the Flying ingot. "But now that you're here, we can use this!"

Dave looked at the glowing ingot as it rested in his hand.

His heart skipped a beat (or, really, several).

His breathing went very shallow.

Like Wall-Walker, the ingot had strange symbols all around it, but in the center of this one was a bumblebee in flight.

Dave could barely believe it.

He was going to *fly*.

"How did you know where to find it?" Dave asked, his voice but a whisper.

"Oh. Well. *Señor*. That is quite a story."

And so, in great (and sometimes exaggerated) detail, Sticky proceeded to tell him the hairy, scary tale of what he'd been through. When he was all done, he said, "But it was worth it, eh, *señor*? Look at you!"

It was true. Dave had never looked happier.

"So," Sticky said, "are you ready to try it?"

Dave nodded. Slowly at first, and then with growing determination.

After all, they had work to do. And knowing Damien Black, he could be sure of one thing.

There was no time to lose.

Chapter 22
ITCHY-YITCHY-YAH-YAH

It was unfortunate for Damien Black that his cunning, clever, and crafty brain had been concentrating wholly and solely on revenge. Had he simply picked up his funkydoodle phone and told Yanko Purran that the potion hadn't worked, the man would surely have brewed him another batch.

Or returned the cash.

The matter would have been resolved quite easily. (And, come to think of it, *solved* as well. Although a money-back guarantee had not been discussed, money-back guarantees usually require the return of unused portions.)

(Or, in this case, *potions*.)

Yanko would have recognized right away that there'd been some sort of switcheroo.

Which then would have cascaded into trouble for Roadrunner Express.

Which then would have led Damien Black within striking distance of one Dave Sanchez.

Instead, Damien got mad and spent all his energies devising a diabolical way to get even.

(With interest, of course.)

It was also unfortunate for Damien Black that he had an irrational fear of curses. Just the thought of another gypsy curse gave him the itchy-yitchy-yah-yahs.

Now, it's a well-known fact that the power of the mind can be either a great healing force or, as in the case of a so-called curse, a self-destructive one. The worried mind will find a way to turn angry words into reality.

Suddenly you become clumsy.

Or sleepless.

Or get the itchy-yitchy-yah-yahs.

You see, a curse will work if you think it will.

It is, in short, all in your head.

So. It was the combination of irrational fear and unnecessary revenge that brought Damien Black and the Bandito Brothers to the edge of Gypsy Town.

It was also the combination of irrational fear and unnecessary revenge that made Damien come up with this particularly elaborate and (quite frankly) outrageous plan.

Damien had outfitted the Bandito Brothers as circus-style gypsies. The bigger two—Tito and Angelo—wore brightly colored knit skullcaps, bright, billowy blouses (Tito's was turquoise, Angelo's was golden), vests with bright (brass) buttons and lots of bric-a-brac, and broad belts that had drinking cups, rabbits' feet, weapon sheaths, (rock-filled) coin bags, and various other clinky-clanky items hanging from them.

Tito carried a hand drum.

Angelo carried a lute.

Pablo, on the other hand, carried a tambourine and was dressed (to his dismay) as a gypsy woman.

"Do I have to, boss?" he'd asked Damien again and again, but it became clear that if he refused to put on the flowing skirt, headdress, jewelry, and scarves, he would be out of the running for the (*ahem*) promotion.

Now, Damien had researched gypsy lore and had gone to great lengths to write a script for the Brothers. (They could not, after all, be trusted to enact his devilishly diabolical plan ad lib.) But because the Brothers could not read the script, Damien had been forced to rig Angelo with an earpiece through which he could feed the script (and also hiss instructions) via the walkie-talkie communicator.

And (as if the three Brothers and their costumes weren't enough) there was one other member of the (fake) gypsy entourage.

It was Rosie, the Brothers' bucktoothed burro.

She, too, was dressed in a festive manner, with a wreath of flowers around her neck and colorful ribbons (and little, tinkly bells) tied to her tail.

Now, why on earth would Damien want to have Rosie there?

The answer is (yet again) quite simple: Tito and Angelo may have been sizeable men, but the two together were still not as strong as a single burro (bucktoothed or otherwise).

Not when it came to pulling a wagon, anyway.

You see, Damien had realized (with a joyful jolt) that Yanko Purran's vardo was a rolling laboratory of potion-making materials.

It had exotic ingredients.

Oddly shaped flasks and a tangly tubed distillery!

And the little cherry on the top of the nefarious plan that Damien had whipped up was that this vardo—this rolling potion wagon—came with its own resident alchemist.

You see, Damien had it on good authority that Yanko Purran was a master potion maker, and Damien believed that the man had simply taken him for someone who could easily be suckered and had tried to pinch a few potion-making pennies.

His payback, then, would be to haul Yanko Purran and his vardo up to Raven Ridge, where he would be kept in a secret (and secluded) cave beneath the mansion. Damien would then make the lousy swindler brew any potion he demanded.

Potions that would equip him with a mighty might.

An awesome brawn!

Potions that would rival the powers of the wristband.

That would, in the end, help him get *back* the wristband.

(Plus, he would never have to pay for potions again!)

It was, undoubtedly, the plan of a madman.

And it was, unfortunately, already well under way.

Chapter 23
AN UNEXPECTED PARADE

While the Bandito gypsies put Damien's elaborate (and cross-dressing) plan into motion, Damien took an alternate route to oversee (or, more accurately, *under*see) the execution of his dirty work.

Damien had no fear of being found (or chased) in these subterranean passageways (better known as the sewer system). And (according to the maps he'd consulted) the system ran under Gypsy Town in precisely the areas he needed it to.

Aboveground, the Bandito Brothers simply walked along, taking left after left as they guided Rosie into the heart of Gypsy Town.

Now, Damien had given his cohorts strict

instructions to move along the streets of Gypsy Town in a lighthearted and casual manner and to sing a merry little song anytime they noticed people watching them. And since the Brothers liked to sing, they imagined people watching them, even when they weren't.

Tito hit the hand drum, Pablo rattled the tambourine, and Angelo played the lute (which, for the record, is not a flute missing its "f" but rather a stringed instrument similar to a guitar).

And as they beat and jangled and strummed, they sang:

> Gypsy friends good fortune share.
> The honored king has sent us here.
> Let swallows sing and cleanse his eyes.
> Lift the curtain, see the skies.

Damien (although not able to carry a tune himself) had written the song, using imagery he'd gleaned from his intense (although miserably mishmashed) research about Romany culture. It had taken him hours upon hours to write the lyrics and the melody (such as it was), and he was quite proud of the end result.

The Brothers, however, thought it stank.

"It doesn't make sense!" Angelo had whispered to Pablo.

"The melody is awful, and it doesn't rhyme right!" Pablo had whispered to Angelo.

"Can we go, 'Ah-reeeeeeeeeeeeeeeeeeeeee-ye-ye-ye-ye-yeeeeeeeeeeeeeee'?" Tito had asked.

"Just sing it like I showed you!" Damien had shouted.

But as the Brothers ambled through Gypsy Town, taking one left turn after another after another, they grew weary of singing the senseless words and decided to switch things up.

Gypsy friends in underwear,
Pick your noses, we won't care!

Swallow snot and cross your eyes,
Clap your clappers in the sky!
Ah-reeeeeeeeeeeeee-ye-ye-ye-yeeeeeeeeeeee!

Now, while the Brothers merrily continued their journey, Damien navigated the inky, stinky sewer system and arrived at the manhole cover on Moongaze Place (which was right at the turnoff to Moongaze Court). He stuck the communicator's antenna up through the crowbar hole and discovered that he was getting great reception. He soon realized, however, that the Brothers were butchering his song. And after listening for a horrified moment, he put his mouth up to the communicator and hissed, "That's not how it goes! Sing it right, you fools!"

"But, boss, the kids love it!" Angelo replied.

Damien recoiled.

"Kids?" he asked. "What kids?"

And then (because Damien found it impossible

to keep his long, pointy nose out of his own business) he pushed up the manhole cover ever so slightly and peeked out.

There was a parade coming his way.

A parade of kids and goats and chickens and dogs, led by his three moronic minions. And the Brothers and kids were all singing at the top of their lungs.

About underwear.

And nose picking!

Like a simmering pot of sinister stew, Damien

spittered and spattered and sputtered under the manhole cover. "You blockheads!" He screeched into the communicator. "What are you doing?"

Now, it had been a long time since the Bandito Brothers had been shown any sort of love, let alone appreciation for a musical performance. So Tito and Angelo (and even Pablo, in his gypsy girl outfit) were eating up the attention.

It reminded them of the parties they used to play in their mariachi days.

The fun they used to have.

So (for once) Angelo didn't apologize or grovel. Instead, he said, "Lighten up, boss! We'll get the job done!" and went on singing about nose picking and underwear.

Well! Damien might have flown into another frothy fury, but as the parade approached, it occurred to him that (preposterous as it was) this might work out. After all, who would stop them if all the children in Gypsy Town were singing and dancing and laughing while the vardo heist was going on? People would assume it was just a friendly frolic. An innocent game. An after-school amusement.

Yes, come to think of it, this tricky tactic would work even better!

(It was, to Damien's warped way of thinking, *his* genius that made it so. *He* was the one who had instructed the Brothers to be lighthearted and casual. *He* was the one who had written the merry tune [ruined as it was]. And *he* was the one who had dressed them in a way that made the whole parade possible!)

"Repeat after me," Damien hissed into the communicator. *"We've come to take the white-eyed one . . ."*

"We've come to take the white-eyed one!" Angelo announced with a grand wave in the air.

"To the great Romany healer!"

"To the great Romany healer!"

"He will be transformed!" Damien hissed.

"He will be transformed!" Angelo repeated (in an accidentally hissy way).

"*Of all those who seek healing,* he *has been chosen!*"

"Of all those who seek healing," Angelo said grandly, "*he* has been chosen!"

Then Damien whispered, "Now. Have Pablo keep him inside—"

"Now!" Angelo announced. "Have Pab—"

"NO, YOU IDIOT!" Damien snapped.

"NO, YOU—" Angelo suddenly caught on and whispered, "Right, right—sorry, boss."

Damien took a deep, angry breath through his long, pointy nose. "You're almost there. Just follow the plan. Contain the blind man, connect the wagon, and move out as fast as you can."

"We're on it, boss!"

And with that, the Bandito Gypsies and their joyful entourage clomped right over the manhole cover and made their final left turn, onto Moongaze Court.

Chapter 24
BUZZY BEE POWER

Meanwhile, in a secluded clearing outside Damien's mansion, Dave was learning to fly.

Or, at least, wobble in the air.

He'd discovered that flying required a running start and a leap into the air, and that once you were airborne, concentrating on going up (or down) and leaning (left or right) controlled the elevation and direction.

However, after the initial rush of being airborne, Dave quickly became frustrated because, try as he might, he was most definitely not darting, or diving, or zooming through space.

And he could only get about five feet off the ground.

"What am I doing wrong?" Dave wailed.

Sticky shook his little gecko head and said, "It's a Buzzy Bee, señor, not a fierce falcon."

"Meaning?"

Sticky gave a little shrug. "This is how a buzzy bee flies?"

Now, it's a well-known fact that when someone makes a beeline, they move lickety-split and get there quick. And although honeybees have been clocked at up to twenty-two miles per hour, bumblebees can only do about ten (and that's when they're in a hurry).

Normally, bumblebees are *not* in a hurry.

Normally, they're hovering around like fuzzy-tummied zeppelins, taking a pinch of pollen here and a nip of nectar there.

Normally, they look like they could very easily fall right out of the sky.

"Are you kidding me?" Dave cried. "This is it?"

"I know that evil *hombre* liked flying, but

I never saw him do it." Sticky shrugged again. "Maybe flap your arms?"

"Flap my arms? I've got to *flap*?"

"I don't know, *señor*. I'm just saying, maybe you could try?"

So Dave (feeling totally and terminally ridiculous) flapped.

Things did not improve.

"Maybe it just takes time to learn?" Sticky suggested when Dave stopped flapping.

Dave wobbled around in the air a bit longer, willing himself to go higher. Faster. But nothing changed. "I could go faster on my bike!" he said at last.

"This is true, *señor*."

"My whole life, I've dreamt about flying . . . but not like this!"

"You'll get better at it, *señor*. But, uh, right now shouldn't we be getting down to help the potion man?"

"Like *this?*" Dave asked.

"Hmm," Sticky said, tapping his chin with a finger. "It might be zippier to take the bike."

Dave landed awkwardly and removed the Flying ingot. "No kidding," he grumbled.

So Dave and Sticky relied on old-fashioned pedal power to leave Raven Ridge. But right before they reached the Moongaze Boulevard turnoff, Dave hid his bike behind some shrubs along Jackaroo Avenue and said, "I have an idea."

"Does it use Flying?"

Dave clicked an ingot into the powerband. "First it uses Wall-Walker."

"See?" Sticky said with a very satisfied look. "Gecko Power is *asombroso!*"

Dave gave him a little smile and then got down to business. "The potion guy lives in a circus trailer in the middle of Gypsy Town. You have to go left, left, left about a hundred times to find it.

I'm thinking if I go diagonal, I can sneak up to it quick and see what's going on. If anything."

"Oh, something's going on, *señor*," Sticky said sagely.

So Dave entered Gypsy Town, zippy-toed up the side of one house, traversed the roof (diagonally), and switched to the Flying ingot. Then he took a running jump (and a leap of faith) from the rooftop and flew like a bony-bodied bumblebee to a neighboring rooftop, where he landed, ran (diagonally) across, and then flew to the next rooftop.

And the next.

And the next.

"*Asombroso!*" Sticky cried as Dave got the hang of it. "I'm a flying leeezard! A flying leeezard!"

The two got to the heart of Moongaze Maze much faster than they would have on Dave's bike, but as they neared Moongaze Court, Dave heard a strange noise and came to a stop. "What *is* that?" he whispered.

"Ay-ay-ay," Sticky moaned. "That's the Brothers. I'd know their singing anywhere!"

"But they're singing about . . . *underwear?*"

Now, you may recall that in this part of Moongaze Maze, the trees and animals seemed to take over. The foliage was fuller. The goats had more horns. There were also birds and snakes and toads and squirrels. It was like a little jungle, really, and when you think of jungles, what one animal always springs to mind?

(Ah, what animal indeed!)

"Eeeeeek-reeeeeeek?" came a cry from across Moongaze Court.

"The *monkey?*" Dave gasped, and flew forward to get a better look.

"Not him!" Sticky groaned when they spotted him at the base of a tree. "Not again!"

It was, indeed, the monkey. (A fact easily

confirmed by the satchel strapped across his chest.) The little rhesus had found refuge from honking horns and angry merchants and rabid animal control agents in this tranquil neighborhood jungle. But as the procession of Bandito Gypsies and kids and goats and dogs turned up Moongaze Court, the monkey shrieked and bounced and pointed.

It was as though he was trying to warn people about the phony gypsies.

It was as if, despite the elaborate costumes, he recognized the Brothers.

Dave soaked in the sight. "Why are they dressed like that? Why did they bring Rosie? What are they *doing?*"

"The big question, *señor,* is where's that evil *hombre?*"

Dave looked around quickly. Sticky was right—the ruthless treasure hunter had to be nearby. What if he already had them in his sights?

Now, while Dave was worried about Damien, and the procession was making its way up Moongaze Court, a cautiously curious six-horned goat approached the monkey from behind. And finding the scent of the satchel quite compelling, the goat became more curious (and less cautious) and began nibbling on the bag with its prehensile lips.

And its tongue.

And its teeth.

The monkey, however, was so intent on eeeking and screeching out a warning that he did not notice the goat, or that it had now ripped a hole in the bottom of the satchel.

Himalayan coffee grounds began pouring out of it.

One ounce.

Two.

Three and four!

And as the grounds ran onto the *ground*, out fell one coffee-dusted squirt-top container.

"Reeeeeeeeek!" the little monkey cried when he noticed that his coffee stash had been compromised. Clutching the hole to stop the flow, he scurried up a tree, leaving the goat to nibble and gnaw (and, yes, puncture) the squirt-top container.

Chapter 25
SHOWDOWN!

While Dave and Sticky watched the Bandito Brothers approach the vardo from a rooftop, Damien Black kept an eye on the action from beneath the manhole cover. And as the parade moved farther and farther from him, Damien found it more and more difficult to *stay* undercover.

Before too long, he had pushed the lid to the side.

Before too long, he had stepped up a few rungs on the portal's metal ladder (which is, in case you didn't know, how city workers get down the manhole to enter the sewer system).

"Get Pablo into the wagon quickly!" Damien hissed into the communicator. "Tell him to silence the gypsy, but nothing more! I need him alive!" Then he grumbled, "At least for now."

"Go!" Angelo commanded Pablo, and (grabbing his skirts so he could move faster) Pablo immediately mounted the vardo's steps and entered without even knocking.

"He's in!" Angelo whispered into the communicator.

"Very good!" Damien replied. "Now announce, 'Rejoice, good Romany people, Yanko Purran is to be healed!'"

Angelo made this announcement (in an exuberant, theatrical manner), then whispered, "Now what?" into the communicator.

"Now hitch up the mule, you fool! Then grab the handles and go!"

So Angelo and Tito removed the vardo's steps and began hitching Rosie to the wagon. But as they did so, a voice boomed down at them from a rooftop nearby.

"STOP! These men are thieves! Don't let them do that!"

"We're not thieves!" Angelo replied, looking around for the source of the accusation.

"We're jolly gypsies!" Tito cried.

Then they saw where the voice had come from. "Oh no!" Angelo gasped. "It's the boy!"

"What?" Damien gasped back through the communicator. "Where?"

"On a roof, boss!" Angelo whispered frantically. "Right next to us!"

The Bandito Brothers had no idea what it was that "the boy" had that Damien wanted. They just knew that Damien wanted whatever it was very, very badly.

They also knew that "the boy" could somehow walk on walls, and because of this, they believed he was bewitched.

Or possessed.

(Or maybe both.)

And now when they saw Dave fly from the neighboring rooftop to the vardo's rooftop, they froze in fear.

"He can *fly?*" Angelo gasped.

"He can *fly,*" Tito confirmed.

Now, had Damien shown some restraint, things might have played out differently. But hearing this unhinged his already precariously hinged mind. "He can FLY?" Damien demanded. "What, exactly, do you mean by 'fly'?"

"Uh," Angelo said, "he can, you know . . . *fly.* Without flapping?"

Damien (who was already half emerged from the sewer system) now leapt to the street. And as he marched toward the vardo, he produced a pistol and shouted, "Just grab the wagon and go!" into the communicator (even though he could be heard perfectly well through the air).

Well! The children and goats and dogs and chickens (and, for that matter, snakes and squirrels

and a certain monkey) had all been startled into a moment of silence when Dave's voice had boomed from the rooftop. But now they noticed an angry-looking man (in a whoosh-swooshy black coat) with a pistol in his hand.

"Hey!" one girl in the gathering called to her friends. "That's the creepy guy I told you about! And he's got a gun!"

The children scattered, hiding behind trees and shrubs, as Damien approached. And Angelo (realizing he was going to lose his promotion if things fell apart) hitched Rosie up to the vardo, grabbed one handle, and barked at Tito to grab the other.

But just as they were pulling the wagon forward (yanking it free from its service connections), Dave flew down from the vardo's roof and hovered above them. "Put it DOWN!" he commanded.

As much as Damien was in a state of disbelief over how Dave had managed to obtain the Flying ingot, he now knew that Dave did, in fact, have it, and the thought of this invasion, this violation, this . . . this *confiscation* made his blood boil.

His veins pop.

His temper snap.

"KEEP MOVING, YOU FOOLS!" Damien shouted. And as Angelo, Tito, and Rosie bolted forward and pulled the vardo down the dirt road, Damien raised his pistol, taking careful aim at Dave.

"*Señor!*" Sticky cried. "He's deadly with that shooter!"

Ah, yes.

Deadly and merciless.

And in his cold, calculating heart, Damien Black had never wanted anything dead as much as he wanted Dave dead.

It wasn't just that it would stop the boy from (yet again) putting a monkey wrench into one of his plans.

It was that killing Dave would deliver a doubly diabolical dividend: The nettling nuisance of a boy would be gone forever, AND he would be able to snatch back the powerband.

A feeling of felonious glee ran through Damien.

A little bwaa-ha-ha bubbled up inside him.

He couldn't have planned this more perfectly if he'd tried!

And so the hard-hearted, cold-blooded demon of a man pulled the trigger.

Which dropped the hammer.

Which hit the percussion cap.

Which ignited the gunpowder.

Which sent a musket ball of solid lead flying straight at Dave.

Chapter 26
A ONE-SIDED DUEL

A bullet fired from a dueling pistol has a muzzle velocity of approximately eight hundred feet per second.

That's more than 545 miles per hour.

(Which, to put things in perspective, is approaching the speed of sound.)

There is no time to react.

No dodging to be done.

You're hit before the sound of the shot even registers in your brain.

So to say that Dave dodged Damien's deadly wad of lead would be to imply that he purposely reacted to the trigger pull and moved to avoid being hit.

He did no such thing.

It was simply his inability to fly in a straight line (or hover in the same spot) that saved his life.

It was, if you will, the bumble in the bee that caused the bullet to blast past him instead of into him.

But hearing the bullet whiz by made Dave lose his levitation concentration, and before long he was frantically flapping, then flailing, and finally falling to the ground.

Dave landed on his arm with a painful thump, and although he broke no bones, the Flying ingot was jarred loose and tumbled from the powerband onto the ground beside him.

In the wink of a deadly eye, Damien was upon him with his second pistol drawn.

"Well, well. See what we have here," he hissed, pinning Dave's arm with one big black boot. Slowly, he reached down and plucked the

Flying ingot from the dirt and slipped it into his coat. "How clever are you now, hmm? You pesky little pickpocket."

Dave's heart hammered in his chest. The children were gone. The vardo was gone. All that remained in the isolated area were Damien and Dave (and, of course, Sticky).

Things had come down to a showdown of good versus evil.

Only in this case, evil held both pistols.

Good, it seemed, was doomed.

"I give myself up!" Sticky said as Damien placed the loaded pistol at Dave's head. "Take the powerband. Take me! Just leave the boy. He only did what I told him to!"

Damien sneered. "I don't need you, you pesk! I'm through with both of you!"

Now, in your life you will have moments where all will seem lost. The good in you will seem completely quashed by forces beyond your control, and it will take every fiber of your being to believe that all is *not* lost, that somehow, someway, you can get out from under the painful pinning of the Boot of Evil.

You *must* make yourself believe.

Around the next corner, past the next bend, at the end of the tunnel, *somewhere*, there is light.

Or help.

Or, in this case, a goat.

A six-horned goat, in fact, that remembered this baaaaaad black-coated human from a previous encounter.

A six-horned goat that was (for reasons it couldn't quite understand) really feeling its oats.

And as Damien held the pistol to Dave's head and (in a classic villainous manner) savored the deliverance of his dastardly revenge, the goat lowered its head and *charged*.

Now, a charging goat goes nowhere near the speed of sound, but before Damien could react to the sound of pounding hooves, the goat butted him from behind.

KA-BLAM! the pistol fired (into the dirt, not Dave).

KA-ZAM! went Dave's and Sticky's eyes as they watched Damien fly through the air.

KA-THONK! Damien landed nearly twenty feet away..

"Quick, *señor!*" Sticky cried. "Get the shooter!"

Dave snatched the pistol from the ground but said, "I don't know how to use it!"

"Just conk him on the *cabeza*! It's only a one-shooter, anyway."

But as Damien attempted to stagger to his feet, the goat (having displayed just a fraction of the Moongaze potion's power) curled a lip and *charged*, butting the wicked villain from (and in the) behind.

Damien flew forward, then tumbled over and over and over (and over and over some more).

"*Ouchie-huahua!*" Sticky cried. "That has got to hurt!"

With the pistol in hand, Dave chased after the villain, determined to not let him get away

(if, that is, he survived his tumbleweed experience).

Damien's trip ended, however, where it had begun.

At the (still open) lid to the sewer system.

(The goat, it seemed, had butted a hole in one.)

And although in tremendous pain and only borderline conscious, Damien managed to grasp the edge of the manhole and growl, "I'll get you, boy!" before he slipped down the hole and disappeared into the stinky river below.

Chapter 27
CIRCLING THE WAGON

After Dave shoved the manhole cover back in place, he put the Wall-Walker ingot in the power-band and rushed off to intercept the Bandito Brothers. And I'd like to report that Gecko Power is what stopped the vardo heist, but it did not.

The children of Moongaze Maze did.

First, there was the matter of the Brothers making a wrong turn.

Then there was the matter of a dead end.

Then there was the ambush of children with jump ropes and baseball bats and rocks.

And as if that weren't enough to control Damien's dead-ended henchmen, there was the small matter of Pablo being tossed from the vardo by the blind (but apparently deft) potion man, causing the children to discover that he was a hairy-legged man.

The jeers and jokes that followed were merciless and set into motion the children circling the wagon, brandishing their weapons, and (most frightening of all to the Brothers) calling for their parents.

Getting no reception from the communicator, Angelo at last shouted, "We give up!" Then the three Brothers abandoned their mission, rushing past Dave and Sticky as they headed for the hills.

Or, rather, the ridge.

Yes, the Brothers may have ditched their gypsy getups, but they did not ditch their boss. They, instead, returned to the mansion to nurse the battered and bruised (and direly dirty) Damien Black back to health.

Pablo and Angelo kept his wounds clean and his bruises iced.

Tito fed him flaky biscuits and crow stew.

(For the record, Damien didn't know it was crow—he thought it tasted like chicken. Although the occasional piece of clinging black fuzz should have given it away.)

Despite eating crow, Damien never actually admitted to the Brothers that he'd done anything wrong. He, instead, blamed them and "the boy" and vowed a comeback. (And although Damien displayed great bravado, his cursed nightmares continued, worsened by the fact that some hairy, scary spiders had made wrong turns in the confounding corridors of his mansion and were now roaming about, looking for something to soupify.)

Rosie (who was apparently the smartest of the bunch) did not return to the mansion. She liked being in the mini jungle of Moongaze Maze, and none of the other animals—not even the potion-powered goat—seemed to mind her. (After three solid days of sleep, the potion-powered goat was confused to see her, but it was confused by a lot of things after that. Besides, it had such a fierce and frightening headache that it couldn't be bothered getting territorial.)

I should also, I suppose, let you know that the

gouges in the Sanchezes' family room ceiling (and wall) were blamed on Evie.

Dave could not believe his ears, as his extremely sly sister never got blamed for anything. But Evie made the mistake of catnapping Topaz from next door (because she really, really, really wanted a kitty of her own). It became clear to Mrs. Sanchez from the cat's screeching and hissing that Evie had tortured the poor feline (which she had, in fact, not), and that the claw marks had come from her swinging the cat by the tail and catapulting her around the room.

The catnapping, of course, gave Lily and her friends something more to tease Dave about, but he just tried to tune them out.

After all, he was the Gecko.

He could walk on walls.

He had *flown*.

(Well, sort of.)

And he and Sticky were tight again.

(Very.)

Sticky had even resumed spending his days at school with Dave, and promised to keep his sticky fingers to himself.

(Or, at least, to try.)

So here we are at the end of the adventure. All the loose ends are tied up and—

What's that?

Oh.

Oh, right.

The monkey.

Well!

The monkey did, in fact, return to Damien's monstrous mansion.

Not to reunite with that deadly, diabolical demon of a man.

Oh no.

He returned because he ran out of coffee. (Or, more accurately, the coffee ran out on him.) And (addict that he was) he decided once again to risk life and limb for a new supply of the good stuff.

Unfortunately for the monkey, Damien had set up an evil-eye monitoring system in his espresso café, and when he saw the monkey pinching the grounds, he hobbled and wobbled through the mansion in time to corner him.

Unfortunately for *Damien*, however, the cornered monkey curled back his lips and flashed a familiar silver and blue grill, shocking Damien so much that he let the monkey get away.

After that, Damien returned to his great room and paced the floorboards (in a stiff, sore, and painfully slow manner), trying to piece everything together and plot a diabolical comeback. When he did, at last, have a tiny little hiccup of a new plan, he hobbled up to his inner sanctum, snatched up his funkydoodle phone, and placed a call to—

Ah, but I'm getting carried away.

I really *must* stop.

Who Damien called and what dastardly, diabolical plan it set into motion is, I'm afraid, a story for another time.

For this story, for today, the time has come to say . . . *adíos!*

A GUIDE TO SPANISH AND STICKYNESE TERMS

adiós (Spanish / *ah-DEE-ohs*): goodbye, see ya later, alligator

amigo (Spanish / *ah-MEE-go*): friend, buddy, pal

ándale (Spanish / *AHN-duh-lay*): hurry up, come on,
    get a move on

asombroso (Spanish / *ah-sohm-BRO-so*): awesome, amazing

ay-ay-ay (Spanish and a Sticky favorite): depending on the
    inflection, this could mean oh brother, oh please, or you
    have *got* to be kidding

ay caramba (Spanish and a Sticky favorite / *ai cah-RAHM-bah*):
    oh wow! or oh brother! or I am not believing this!

ay chihuahua (Stickynese / *ai chee-WAH-wah*): oh man, oh no

bobo (Spanish / *BO-bo*): dumb, foolish, silly

cabeza (Spanish / *cah-BAY-thah*): head

estúpido (Spanish / *eh-STOO-pee-do*): stupid

excelente picante (Spanish and Stickynese / *ex-sel-EN-tay
    pee-CAHN-tay*): excellent and spicy hot!

fieras (Spanish / *fee-EH-rahs*): wild animals, beasts

freaky frijoles (Stickynese / *free-HO-lays*): literally, weird beans.
    But for Sticky, oh wow or how strange

gata (Spanish / *GAH-tauh*): female cat

genio beanio (Stickynese / *hay-nee-oh BEE-nee-oh*): genius!

híjole (Spanish / *HEE-ho-lay*): wow!

holy tacarole / holy guaca-tacarole (Stickynese / *gwah-cuh-tah-cuh-RO-lee*): holy smokes!

hombre (Spanish / *AHM-bray*): man, dude

horroroso (Spanish / *hor-or-OH-so*): horrible, terrifying, awful

lobo (Spanish / *LO-bo*): wolf

loco (Spanish / *LO-co*): crazy, loony

loco-berry burritos (Stickynese): literally, crazy-berry rolled tortilla sandwiches. But for Sticky, extra-specially crazy

matón (Spanish / *mah-TONE*): bully, tough guy

mi'jo (Spanish / *MEE-ho*): dear, my darling boy. For a girl, you'd say *mi'ja* (*MEE-ha*)

morrocotudo (Spanish / *mor-ro-co-TOO-do*): fabulous, wonderful

pistola (Spanish / *pees-TOH-la*): pistol, gun

ratero (Spanish / *rah-TAIR-oh*): thief

señor (Spanish / *SEN-yohr*): mister

sí (Spanish / *see*): yes

vámonos (Spanish / *VAH-mo-nohs*): let's go!

zonzo (Spanish / *SOHN-so*): stupid, dumb

WENDELIN VAN DRAANEN has been everything from a forklift driver to a high school teacher but is now enjoying life as a full-time writer. She is the author of the Shredderman quartet, the Sammy Keyes mysteries, and many other novels.

Ms. Van Draanen lives with her husband and two sons in central California. Her hobbies include the "three R's": reading, running, and rock 'n' roll.

STEPHEN GILPIN developed a taste for drawing strange things at an early age and hasn't looked back since. He graduated with honors from New York City's School of Visual Arts, where he studied painting and cartooning. He currently lives in Hiawatha, Kansas, with his wife and their four children.